AN ALPENGLOW RIDGE NOVEL

Hope by the Horizon

ZEA KAYLEIGH GALAN

To You,
The right time is
when it's time,
not when you want it to be.

Playlist

Sophia Scott – Mullet Over
Reyna Roberts – He Gon' Be A Problem
Tyler Hubbard – Wish You Would
Kasey Tyndall – Bad For Me
Chase McDaniel – Project
BRELAND – For What It's Worth
Dallas Smith – Fixer Upper
Faren Rachels – Hard Headed Heart
Alana Springsteen – look i like
Mike Parker – Love You On My Mind
Justin Champagne, VK – It's You

AN ALPENGLOW RIDGE NOVEL

Hope by the Horizon

CHAPTER 1

Cammie Clyfford

"TODAY IS GOING TO be a good day."

Repeating the phrase in my head, I adjust my wide-brimmed hat, shielding my eyes from the mid-morning sun. I woke up with a feeling like my day would need a little extra manifestation for calm.

It's going to be a good day.

I walk the familiar path toward Mason Sanctuary, nestled in Alpenglow Ridge, Colorado. The ranch it's a part of has been my home since I moved here from Portland five years ago.

Reese Mason, the owner of Mason Ranch and a good friend of mine, stands by the paddock, her dark hair tied back and her signature red cowboy boots catching the sunlight. Reese has always been a commanding presence, tall and confident, with a gaze that can unearth the truth from anyone. She did not play about her business and everyone knows it. It was easy for me to trust her when we met and the biggest reason why she's my friend.

"Morning, Cammie," Reese calls out, her voice warm. "Got your work cut out for you today."

I nod, my curly afro bouncing around my face with the movement. "Wouldn't have it any other way. How's Honey Bee doing?"

Reese's expression softens. "Still skittish, but she's eating again. I'm hoping you can work your magic." Honey Bee, a chestnut mare with a streak of stubbornness, is my latest challenge. Reese personally purchased the horse from someone in town who couldn't handle her and isolated her for most of her life. With little human interaction and very little interaction with other horses in her small living area, she had become distrusting of many things that should be commonplace for her.

I smile, knowing that I did have something like a magic touch when it came to the horses.

"Wind's blowing in some extra help for you too. *Surprise!* It'll be nice for you to have someone else around to help with the horses since I'm stepping back this summer. He knows what he's doing. "

"He? Who is it, Reese?" I raise a very skeptical brow at her before crossing my arms over my chest. Something tells me that whatever her surprise is, it will not lend well to my *good day* mantra.

"If I told you, it wouldn't be a very good surprise, now would it?" She chuckles and hops onto her own horse, Heather, to ride back to the main house.

"I don't like the sound of that," I call after her, but I know she doesn't hear me since she's already halfway across the pasture.

My role as director and the only hippotherapist at Mason Sanctuary has allowed me to connect deeply with the horses, using my background in therapeutic riding to help them and the children who come here for sessions. It's my happy place.

The sanctuary always smells of hay, sunshine, and earth after the morning chores, a comforting scent that makes the place feel alive. I'm in the middle of adjusting a saddle on Honey Bee, when I hear the familiar sound of boots on gravel. But this time, it's not the usual shuffle of a volunteer or the soft steps of a client and their parent. These footsteps are heavier, deliberate. I glance up, and there he is—Ellis McNair.

My surprise, I'm guessing.

The man's voice calls into the building, "The fun has arrived!"

He strides in like he owns the place, the sunlight catching the warm brown of his skin and glinting off the buckle of his belt. His eyes scan the paddock, dark and piercing, before they land on me.

Sade's *Smooth Operator* plays in my mind as time slows for his entrance. I can't think straight with him swaggering in like every woman's wet dream.

Maybe just mine.

My stomach twists in that stupid, predictable way it always does when I see him. *Five years.* That's how long I've been watching him, mostly from a distance. Ellis—the town's favorite cowboy and serial flirt—the man who could charm his way out of a speeding ticket with nothing more than a lopsided grin. I've seen him work his magic on half the women in town, each one leaving with stars in their eyes and stories to tell.

And yet, here he is, standing in front of me like he has any business being in my world, *again.*

A few months ago, Tony, the ranch manager, delegated Ellis and Taylor to help out in Mason Sanctuary while we worked on getting more volunteers here. Mason Ranch is a working cattle ranch, but it also offers horse boarding, children's camps, riding clinics and, now, hippotherapy.

As the only non-profit operation on the land, Reese has been very selective on how many people she allows me to employ, and that each employee can offer a special skill that we truly need. Caring for horses is no cheap task but many of the volunteers here have their own reasons for joining our team. *That's how I got here.* Once Reese got everything set up, there was no need for the cowboys to come over to this side of Mason Ranch.

Or so I thought.

"Cammie," he says, his voice low and easy, the kind of voice that feels like it's wrapping itself around you. *Too sensual and too close.* "Heard you might need an extra set of hands around here."

His hands, I need. I need them around my—

Mentally, I stop that train of thought right where it started. If he's here, then he's my new employee for all intents and purposes. *I'm his boss.* There is nowhere that those thoughts can go.

I raise an eyebrow, refusing to let my lust betray me. "And who told you that?" I already know the answer to that question but I ask anyway, hoping to give my brain a little more time to work properly with his alluring presence near me.

"Does it matter?" He shrugs, his grin creeping up like he knows exactly how disarming it is. *I know he does.* "Figured I'd come see if I could help out until they add me back to payroll at the Ranch. Besides, it's been a minute since I've been around horses. Thought it'd be nice to get back in the saddle."

I almost laugh. *Nice?* Since when does Ellis do anything because it's nice? Instant gratification is his game and he plays it well.

"You don't exactly scream 'volunteer' material," I say, turning back to the saddle. Honey Bee flicks her ears, sensing my tension. I run a hand down her neck to soothe her, to soothe myself.

"Maybe not," he admits, leaning casually against the gate. "But I've got extra time and energy to burn. You could use the help, couldn't you?" Flirting rolls off his tongue as easy as it probably is for him to breathe. I feel like a teenage girl with no experience dealing with men near him. *I'm not that girl* and I won't allow him to fluster me.

If I say it enough times, maybe we'll both believe it.

I glance at him again, this time longer than I mean to. His short, tightly coiled curls sit neatly atop his head, the deep black color catching the light in subtle glints. The sides are tapered, fading smoothly into his natural skin tone. His shirt is fitted just enough to hint at the strength beneath, and the way he's standing there, so relaxed and self-assured, makes it hard to think straight. I wonder, offhandedly, what products he uses that make his hair look good even after taking a hat on and off all day.

I've spent years keeping my distance from him, keeping myself safe. Because Ellis is exactly the kind of man who could break a woman's heart without even meaning to.

I've already had my fill of heartbreak.

But there's something different in his eyes today, something I can't quite place. It's not just the playful glint I've seen a hundred times before. There's a steadiness, a seriousness, as if he's trying to tell me this isn't a joke to him. "Look, I know you don't trust me," he says, his voice softer now. "And I get it. But I'm here. Just give me a chance to prove I'm not as bad as everybody says I am, huh?"

The air feels heavy between us, like the universe is holding its breath.

"Fine," I say finally, against my better judgment. "But if you mess up, you're out. The last thing I need is someone getting in the way."

His grin returns, wider this time, and for a second, I almost regret saying yes. *Almost.*

"Deal," he says, tipping his hat. "Where do I start, boss?"

I do not like the way that sounds.

I don't.

I *don't.*

I gesture toward the tack room, trying to ignore the flutter in my chest. "Grab a brush. Let's see if you can manage to groom a horse without getting kicked today."

As he walks away, I take a deep breath, trying to steady myself. *This is a mistake.* It has to be.

Honey Bee snorts softly as I approach her again, large brown eyes wary but curious. I move slowly, speaking in soothing tones as I extend my hand. The mare hesitates before nudging my palm, a small victory that makes my heart swell.

"Good girl," I murmur, stroking her neck. "We're going to take this one step at a time."

I spend the next hour working with her, guiding her through gentle groundwork exercises to rebuild trust. If I can get her to trust me, then I can get her to start trusting other riders and maybe work with some of the kids who are more experienced. She's a ways off from that kind of responsibility, but I have goals for her. I believe she can reach them.

By the time I'm done, I'm sweating from working in the summer heat but satisfied. I wipe my brow and step out of the stall, nearly colliding with a hard chest. I put my hands out in front of me to catch myself and pull them back immediately when I notice who it is. "Sorry," I say, startled.

"Didn't mean to sneak up on you," Ellis winks, holding up his hands. "How's Honey Bee?"

"Progressing," I say, my tone cautious. "She's still wary, but she's getting there."

Ellis nods, his expression thoughtful. "Reese was right to bring you in. You've got a knack for this."

The compliment catches me off guard, and I'm not sure how to respond. "Thanks," I say finally, but the silence lingers for a while after that. I don't fill it, choosing caution over falling into whatever flirtation he could be setting up right now.

"You've been here a while now," Ellis says, breaking the silence. "Do you miss the PNW?"

I pause, considering his question. I didn't even know he knew where I was from. "Sometimes," I admit. "Portland's nice. The rain, the culture, the forests... But there's something about this place that feels more like home."

Ellis glances at me, his expression unreadable. "It's not for everyone."

"What about you?" I ask, curious. "Have you always been here?"

He nods. "Born and raised. Left for a bit, but this place has a way of pulling you back and here I am."

There's a weight to his words, a hint of a story I don't dare press for. Maybe that's the reason why he stopped working the ranch for so long. *And maybe that's why he's back now.*

He's watching me, that infuriatingly amused expression on his face, all hints of his earlier enigmatic mood gone. His smug grin is back, since he knows exactly how to get under my skin—and enjoys doing it. "Did you want something?" I ask.

"Nah... You sure you're not secretly a city girl who just *likes* to play dress-up in boots?" he asks, his grin wide and teasing.

I pause mid-stroke, glancing over my shoulder at him with a deadpan look. "You're really a charmer, aren't you?"

He laughs, a deep, rich sound that seems to vibrate in the air between us. "I'm being honest," he says, holding up his hands as if to defend himself. "I could tell from the way you walked into town—you've got that 'don't mess with me' vibe."

I roll my eyes, turning back to Honey Bee, who seems far more tolerable than the man currently pestering me. "I don't need to prove anything to you," I mutter under my breath, focusing on my task.

Ellis, of course, doesn't let it drop. He steps closer, his voice dropping just enough to make my pulse skip. "I wasn't asking you to prove anything," he says, his tone laced with that maddening smirk. "Just enjoying the view."

I turn to face him fully this time, crossing my arms over my chest. His grin widens, like he's won some unspoken game, and I hate that my cheeks feel a little warmer than they should.

"Keep staring, cowboy," I say, matching his playful tone with one of my own. "You might just learn something you weren't expecting."

For a moment, he looks like he might have a quick comeback, but instead, he chuckles and shakes his head, stepping back with a mock salute. "Fair enough," he says, his voice tinged with amusement.

As he moves on to grab a bridle from the tack room, I let out a breath I didn't realize I was holding. He's trouble—I've known that from the start. But as I watch him roll up his sleeves and get to work, I can't help but wonder if trouble might not be such a bad thing after all.

* * *

LATER THAT EVENING, AS I sit on the porch of my small cabin overlooking the pasture, I can't shake the feeling that today did not go how I planned. It wasn't a good day but it wasn't bad either. It was simply different. The ranch, with its sprawling pastures and openness, has been a place of solace for me. But now, it feels like something else.

Ellis's words replay in my mind, his presence lingering like the warmth of the setting sun. For the first time in a long while, I allow myself to wonder what it would be like to let someone in—to share the quiet beauty of this life with another person even if just for a short time.

As the stars begin to twinkle above Alpenglow Ridge, I make a silent promise to myself to stay open to the possibilities this place has to offer. Because maybe, just maybe, the ranch isn't the *only thing* capable of healing.

CHAPTER 2

Ellis McNair

"MORNING," I CALL OUT, hopping down from my horse, Rebel.

I tighten the straps on the saddle, my hands moving on autopilot while my mind churns. The air is crisp this morning. The kind of weather that makes the mountains around Alpenglow Ridge glow gold in the early light. The rhythmic clink of tools and the soft shuffle of hooves fill the space and low chatter, a familiar soundtrack to my life again. Out in the paddock, I catch sight of Cammie leading Honey Bee through another session.

She moves with purpose, her athletic frame relaxed but focused. She's dressed in a pair of well-fitted denim jeans, a soft, burnt-orange button-down shirt with the sleeves rolled up to her elbows, and scuffed brown work boots. Her curly afro with soft, springy curls that frame her face and cascade down to her shoulders held back with a headband to keep stray curls out of her eyes as she works. I haven't failed to notice how beautiful Cameron Clyfford is. But she doesn't use that beauty like a weapon or even seem to use it *at all*.

I think that makes her even more beautiful.

The horses respond to her in a way that feels almost magical. Watching her work, I can't help but feel a tug of something deeper. *Respect? Admiration? Maybe more than I'm ready to admit about my new boss.*

Cammie keeps her walls high, and I'm still figuring out how to scale them.

Cammie glances up, her expression careful. "Morning. Didn't expect to see you here today."

"Reese sent me with some supplies," I say, gesturing to the truck bed. "Figured I'd drop them off and see if you needed anything else today."

She nods, her eyes flicking briefly to mine before returning to Honey Bee. "Thanks. We've been running low on blankets and the rest." She takes the saddle and pad off of the mare and begins brushing her coat.

"Noticed," I reply, grabbing the package again and hefting it onto my shoulder. "Figured you'd need them sooner rather than later."

Cammie pauses, her brush hovering mid-air. For a second, I think she's going to say something, but then she just nods again.

The thing about Cammie is—she's hard to read. Most folks around here wear their emotions like a badge, but she's different. *Guarded.* Like she's holding back some part of herself, even when she's smiling. And for reasons I can't quite explain, I want to know what's behind that wall.

"You're looking a little too serious today," I tease upon returning from putting the supplies away. "Can't handle the dry Colorado heat, huh?"

She doesn't even glance at me. "I'm doing just fine without your distractions."

Her tone is sharp, but I don't take it personally. That edge of hers only makes me want to dig deeper. I step closer, lowering my voice. "That's what you think. But you've been distracting me ever since I walked over here."

That gets her attention. She straightens, her hand pausing from whatever notes she was writing. "Don't say things like that," she says, her voice tight.

I offer a soft smile, leaning casually against the fence. "I'll say whatever I want, especially when it's true."

Her eyes narrow, but I catch the faintest flicker of uncertainty, maybe even curiosity. She doesn't reply, just turns back to her notes, her movements a little more hurried than before.

I know I'm lingering longer than I probably should but still I nod toward the mare. "You've got a way with her," I say.

Cammie glances at me, her brow furrowed. "It's not magic though some-times it feels like it. Just time and trust."

"Still," I say, crossing my arms. "Not everyone can do what you do."

Her lips twitch like she's fighting a smile, but she doesn't let it break through. "Guess it's easier for me to work with the horses than the people."

That lands heavier than she probably intended, and I'm not sure what to say to that. Before I can think of a response, one of the sanctuary volunteers, Erin, walks over, calling my name.

"Ellis! You're a lifesaver," she says with a grin. "Reese told me you'd be bringing the blankets. Thanks a million!"

"No problem," I reply, scratching the back of my neck. The woman keeps talking, something about how the sanctuary's lucky to have me around now, and I chuckle at her over-the-top praise. "Just helping where I can," I say, trying to downplay it.

When I glance back at Cammie, she's focused on Honey Bee again, her shoulders stiff. It's like she's shut me out completely, and I don't understand why.

Anna, a ranch hand, and me are working side by side, stacking hay bales in the corner later in the day. She hums softly as she works, the sound blending with the rhythmic shuffle of hay.

"You're quick," I say, adjusting one of the bales to make the stack sturdier.

Anna glances over, a playful smirk on her lips. "You saying I'm better at this than you?"

I chuckle. "Just saying you've got a knack for it."

As we continue I catch sight of Craig, another ranch hand I used to work with, passing by with a saddle slung over his shoulder. His pace slows for just a moment, his eyes flicking toward us before he moves on. There's no comment, just a brief pause that feels weighted, though I can't quite put my finger on why. *Who pissed in his cheerios?*

By the time I'm back at the main barn, the unease in my gut has only grown. I replay the morning over and over, trying to figure out where I went wrong. *Maybe I shouldn't have lingered. Maybe I shouldn't have laughed with Erin.* Hell, maybe I shouldn't have gone over to the sanctuary at all. I could've stayed at home and not put my foot in my mouth or whatever it was that set Cammie on edge.

But as I start tending to the other chores piling up around the barn, I can't shake the feeling that I'm missing something. *Something important.*

Cammie's not just another face around here. She's got this fire, this drive, that makes you want to step up your game. And even though she's got her walls up, I've seen glimpses of what's underneath in the past. I just don't know if she'll ever let me close enough to really see it. And I want to see it *real bad.*

For now, all I can do is keep showing up. Because if there's one thing I've learned about this life, it's that trust isn't given—it's earned. And if I'm lucky, maybe one day, she'll let me earn hers.

THE NEXT FEW WEEKS pass in a blur of work. I make a point to offer my help where I can—fixing the fencing near the sanctuary, hauling supplies, even sticking around to watch her hippotherapy sessions.

But every time I try to get closer, she pulls away.

Today, it's no different.

I find her in the barn, checking on Blossom. I was sidewalking her when something set her off. The mare panicked too close to the barbwire and got a nasty gash on her hind leg. I was able to get her cleaned up and in her stall, but the damage was done. Blossom is such a kind spirit, it broke my heart to see her in pain.

Cammie's crouched in the stall now, her hands gentle but firm as she inspects her bandages.

"You should be careful," I say from the entryway. "The mare's a little more temperamental today."

She doesn't look up. "I've got it handled. Don't worry."

I step closer, my tone firm. "It's not about worrying, it's about not taking risks you don't need to take."

This time, she glances up, her expression defensive. "I'm not some fragile thing, Ellis. I'm a professional and I can take care of myself."

I crouch down, meeting her gaze head-on. My voice softens to almost a whisper. "I know. But I don't want you to get hurt. Not by the horses... and not by—" I trail off before saying the one person that I likely should have named, *me*. Instead I say, "not by anyone else."

Her eyes widen slightly, and for a moment, I think she's going to say something. Maybe she knew I meant *me*, too. But then she looks away, busying herself with the bandages. "You don't have to worry about that either," she says, her tone clipped.

I nod, standing and stepping back. "Fair enough," I say, though the words feel hollow.

Later that day, I find myself near the paddock, watching Cammie work with the children in her program. She's in her element, her laughter light and contagious as she guides the kids through their group exercises.

It's hard not to admire her. She's strong, determined, and fiercely independent—everything I've always respected in a person. But there's a softness there too, hidden beneath her sharp edges.

Foolishly, I'm still hoping she'll let me close enough to see it.

As the sun sets over Mason Ranch, I make a silent promise to myself: I'm not giving up. Cammie may have her guard up, but I've got time—and patience. And if there's one thing I've learned out here, it's that the best things in life are worth waiting for.

CHAPTER 3

Cammie

"EASY, GIRL! IT'S OKAY," comes my friend's voice from the paddock.

Honey Bee's whinny is sharp, a cry of distress that I can't ignore. By the time I get there, Reese is already holding the mare's reins, her expression tight as she focuses on the horse. Reese was one of the horse trainers here before she took over the Ranch from her dad. She has experience with unruly equines so I trust that she is capable of helping Honey Bee and protecting herself. Either way, I'm sprinting over to the stall to see what is happening.

"She slipped in the mud," Reese says when I reach them, her voice calm though laced through with panic. "Took a bad step coming out of the stall. She was behaving strangely all morning, like she's drunk. Something was wrong before she even took that step."

Drunk?

I kneel beside Honey Bee, running my hands gently down her foreleg. The mare's muscles twitch under my touch, and I feel the telltale heat of an injury. *My heart sinks.* Honey Bee was making good progress. An injury could set her back in a big way.

"We'll need to keep her off this leg," I say, standing up. "Don't want to take any chances. I'll call the vet, but for now, we'll have to adjust."

"Adjust how?" Reese asks, crossing her arms. "You've got three sessions lined up today, and you're short on time as it is."

Before I can answer, Ellis appears, his broad frame cutting an imposing figure as he approaches. His hat is tilted back, and there's a smudge of dirt on his jaw that somehow only makes him look more capable.

"What's going on?" he asks, his voice steady.

"Honey Bee's out," Reese explains. "Cammie's going to need some help rearranging the schedule or with some of her tasks for the day."

Ellis's gaze shifts to me, his dark eyes thoughtful. "What do you need?"

I'm caught off guard by his directness. "I... I need to figure out which horses can afford to have less time with me today. And I'll need help prepping them."

"I've got time," he says simply, as if it's the most natural thing in the world. "Just tell me what to do, boss."

❦

ELLIS AND I WORK side by side in the barn, the air thick with the scent of hay and leather. I'm used to doing this alone, but having him here—lifting saddles, calming the horses—is a strange comfort. He moves with an ease that's both reassuring and maddening, like he's been doing this his whole life. Which I guess, he has since he was a hand long before I moved here.

"You really think you can handle all this work?" I ask, glancing at him as I tighten a strap. "Reese told me that you're back to working the main barn, too."

Ellis steps away from Willow for a moment to look me over, a smirk playing on his lips. "You think I can't handle it?"

He's wearing a lightweight, short-sleeved plaid shirt in muted shades of blue and tan, unbuttoned at the top to reveal a hint of his brown skin. The shirt is tucked neatly into his dark, well-worn jeans, which fit his strong legs perfectly over his work boots. The man looks like cowboy perfection and it's doing *something* to me. There is too much goodness to look at–or more accurately, not get distracted by.

I clear my throat. "Going from not working to working and volunteering here is more than a day's work. You won't have the ability to stand-up right after a while."

"I'm not scared of a little hard work." He winks, "Working hard keeps me strong."

"But it's not about being strong. What we do here is about patience and understanding. Two things that can't come easily if you're exhausted."

He steps closer, his voice low and teasing. "I've got patience. It's one of my many virtues."

I raise an eyebrow, refusing to look at him. "Is that so?"

"If you want," he says, leaning in slightly, "I can show you how patient I really am."

The heat rises to my cheeks, and I take a step back, flustered. "Maybe keep your virtues to yourself, cowboy."

Ellis chuckles. "You might change your mind."

Despite his teasing, Ellis proves to be invaluable. He handles the horses with a care I hadn't expected, his strong hands gentle as he soothes them into their new roles. By the time the first therapy session begins, the uncertainty I had after Blossom's injury has settled into a manageable throb of unease.

That's two horses who had injured themselves in ways that are unlikely for them. Blossom is such a sweet girl, she is the most well behaved of our mares. Ellis's account of what happened just doesn't seem like her. And then Honey Bee... Reese is as close with her as I am. She thought she was acting drunk! What is that even about? I sweep all of those concerns to the back of my mind to focus on the task in front of me.

My first client, Max, sits stiffly in the saddle atop Willow. His hands grip the reins tightly, his knuckles white against the leather. Willow stands patiently, her ears flicking as if she's listening for my next cue. Max has been coming to the sanctuary for six weeks now, but trust doesn't come easily to him. Diagnosed with autism spectrum disorder, he struggles with sensory overload and new environments, and today he seems especially tense. *I hope he's not picking that up from me.*

"Okay, Max," I say softly, stepping up to his side. "Let's start with some deep breaths. Remember how we practiced last time?"

Max glances down at me, his expression tight. His mom stands nearby, watching with a mix of hope and anxiety.

"In through your nose," I demonstrate, taking a deep breath and letting it out slowly. "And out through your mouth. Willow's going to feel it if you relax."

Max hesitates but follows my lead, his shoulders lowering just a fraction as he exhales. Willow shifts her weight, sensing the change in his posture.

"Good job," I say, smiling. "Now let's try a little movement. We'll go slow, just a walk."

I give Willow a gentle pat and click my tongue, and she begins to move, her hooves crunching softly on the gravel. Max tenses again, his body rigid in the saddle.

"Keep breathing, Max," I remind him. "Willow's got you. She's like a big, fluffy grey pillow, remember?"

That earns the smallest twitch of a smile from him. Last week, I'd joked that Willow was softer than his favorite blanket, and he'd seemed to like that.

As Willow takes a few more steps, I notice Max's grip on the reins start to loosen. His shoulders aren't quite as hunched, and he's beginning to move with the horse's rhythm, however slightly.

"Do you want to try steering?" I ask, keeping my tone light and encouraging.

Max doesn't answer right away, but after a moment, he nods. I show him how to hold the reins just so, guiding Willow gently to the left and then to the right. He mimics my movements, tentative at first, but his confidence grows with each turn.

"You're doing it, Max!" I cheer. "Look at you—Willow's listening to you."

A small, proud smile breaks across his face, and for a moment, I see a glimmer of the confidence he's working so hard to build.

After a few laps around the ring, I stop Willow and reach one hand into my pocket for a cut piece of carrot and one of our sensory tools—a soft, colorful scarf. "Ready for a game?" I ask, holding it up.

Willow crunches the carrot while Max eyes the scarf warily. "What kind of game?"

"Let's see if you can wave this while Willow walks," I explain. "It'll help you practice balance and get used to moving your arms while you ride."

He hesitates, but eventually reaches for the scarf. I hand it to him, showing him how to hold it properly.

"Okay, just like before," I say. "Take a deep breath, and let's try a few steps."

Willow starts to walk again, and Max lifts the scarf, letting it flutter in the breeze. At first, his movements are stiff, but as he gains confidence, he starts to wave it more freely.

"Great job, Max!" I say, clapping lightly. "Willow loves how you're leading her."

Max beams, his earlier tension melting away. By the end of the session, he's steering Willow confidently and waving the scarf like a victory flag.

As I help him dismount, his mom approaches, her eyes glistening with unshed tears. "Thank you, Cammie," she says, her voice trembling. "I haven't seen him smile like that in months."

"It's all Max," I reply, glancing at him as he strokes Willow's neck. "He's the one doing the work."

Max looks up at me, his expression shy but proud. "Can I ride Willow again next time?"

"Of course," I say, my heart swelling. "She'll be waiting for you."

As I lead Willow back to the barn, I can't help but feel a deep sense of fulfillment. These moments—watching kids like Max find their confidence, their joy—is why I do this. It's not just therapy—it's a connection, a bridge to something bigger.

And for Max, today wasn't just a ride. It was a step toward trusting the world a little more.

Max's mother looks on with tears in her eyes as he reaches out to stroke the horse's mane. Max has come so far in the time I've been working with him. Nothing is more rewarding than moments just like this one.

"You're good at this," Ellis says, coming to stand beside me. His voice is softer, free of the playful edge.

"Thank you for your help with Willow earlier today," I tell him.

He glances at me, a flicker of something unspoken passing between us. "Just doing what needs to be done."

<hr>

FOR A MOMENT, I let myself relax, the weight of the day lifting slightly now that it's over. But then I hear laughter coming from the parking area out front, a light, feminine sound that sets my teeth on edge. I turn to see one of Ellis's exes, Lena, leaning against his truck, her smile radiant as she waves to him. He grins back, his posture easy, and the sight twists something deep in my chest.

"Looks like you've got company," I say, my voice cool.

Ellis follows my gaze, his expression shifting to confusion. "Lena? She's just..."

"You don't have to explain," I cut him off, turning away. "Don't forget to fill out your timesheet before you leave, for Reese's records."

I don't wait for his response. Instead, I head back to my office, the familiar ache of disappointment settling in. I should've known better than to let my guard down. People like Ellis don't change—not for someone like me, anyway.

That night, as I sit on my porch and watch the stars, I try to shake the day's events from my mind. The ranch is quiet now, the only sounds are the rustle of leaves and the distant call of an owl. But my thoughts are anything but peaceful.

Ellis had shown me a side of himself I hadn't seen before—kind, attentive, and unexpectedly patient. For a brief moment, I'd allowed myself to believe that maybe, just maybe, he could be more than the playboy everyone knows him to be.

But then Lena showing up had reminded me of the truth. Ellis McNair is a man who knows how to make women feel special, but that doesn't mean he's serious. And I *can't afford* to be anyone's passing fancy.

As the night deepens, I make a silent vow to myself: to keep my focus on the work that matters and the people who truly need me. Because no matter how patient Ellis claims to be, I can't risk letting my heart get trampled again.

"Easy, girl! It's okay," comes my friend's voice from the paddock.

Honey Bee's whinny is sharp, a cry of distress that I can't ignore. By the time I get there, Reese is already holding the mare's reins, her expression tight as she focuses on the horse. Reese was one of the horse trainers here before she took over the Ranch from her dad. She has experience with unruly equines so I trust that she is capable of helping Honey Bee and protecting herself. Either way, I'm sprinting over to the stall to see what is happening.

"She slipped in the mud," Reese says when I reach them, her voice calm though laced through with panic. "Took a bad step coming out of the stall. She was behaving strangely all morning, like she's drunk. Something was wrong before she even took that step."

Drunk?

I kneel beside Honey Bee, running my hands gently down her foreleg. The mare's muscles twitch under my touch, and I feel the telltale heat of an injury. *My heart sinks.* Honey Bee was making good progress. An injury could set her back in a big way.

"We'll need to keep her off this leg," I say, standing up. "Don't want to take any chances. I'll call the vet, but for now, we'll have to adjust."

"Adjust how?" Reese asks, crossing her arms. "You've got three sessions lined up today, and you're short on time as it is."

Before I can answer, Ellis appears, his broad frame cutting an imposing figure as he approaches. His hat is tilted back, and there's a smudge of dirt on his jaw that somehow only makes him look more capable.

"What's going on?" he asks, his voice steady.

"Honey Bee's out," Reese explains. "Cammie's going to need some help rearranging the schedule or with some of her tasks for the day."

Ellis's gaze shifts to me, his dark eyes thoughtful. "What do you need?"

I'm caught off guard by his directness. "I... I need to figure out which horses can afford to have less time with me today. And I'll need help prepping them."

"I've got time," he says simply, as if it's the most natural thing in the world. "Just tell me what to do, boss."

<hr>

ELLIS AND I WORK side by side in the barn, the air thick with the scent of hay and leather. I'm used to doing this alone, but having him here—lifting saddles, calming the horses—is a strange comfort. He moves with an ease that's both reassuring and maddening, like he's been doing this his whole life. Which I guess, he has since he was a hand long before I moved here.

"You really think you can handle all this work?" I ask, glancing at him as I tighten a strap. "Reese told me that you're back to working the main barn, too."

Ellis steps away from Willow for a moment to look me over, a smirk playing on his lips. "You think I can't handle it?"

He's wearing a lightweight, short-sleeved plaid shirt in muted shades of blue and tan, unbuttoned at the top to reveal a hint of his brown skin. The shirt is tucked neatly into his dark, well-worn jeans, which fit his strong legs perfectly over his work boots. The man looks like cowboy perfection and it's doing *something* to me. There is too much goodness to look at—or more accurately, not get distracted by.

I clear my throat. "Going from not working to working and volunteering here is more than a day's work. You won't have the ability to stand-up right after a while."

"I'm not scared of a little hard work." He winks, "Working hard keeps me strong."

"But it's not about being strong. What we do here is about patience and understanding. Two things that can't come easily if you're exhausted."

He steps closer, his voice low and teasing. "I've got patience. It's one of my many virtues."

I raise an eyebrow, refusing to look at him. "Is that so?"

"If you want," he says, leaning in slightly, "I can show you how patient I really am."

The heat rises to my cheeks, and I take a step back, flustered. "Maybe keep your virtues to yourself, cowboy."

Ellis chuckles. "You might change your mind."

Despite his teasing, Ellis proves to be invaluable. He handles the horses with a care I hadn't expected, his strong hands gentle as he soothes them into their new roles. By the time the first therapy session begins, the uncertainty I had after Blossom's injury has settled into a manageable throb of unease.

That's two horses who had injured themselves in ways that are unlikely for them. Blossom is such a sweet girl, she is the most well behaved of our mares. Ellis's account of what happened just doesn't seem like her. And then Honey Bee... Reese is as close with her as I am. She thought she was acting drunk! What is that even about? I sweep all of those concerns to the back of my mind to focus on the task in front of me.

My first client, Max, sits stiffly in the saddle atop Willow. His hands grip the reins tightly, his knuckles white against the leather. Willow stands patiently, her ears flicking as if she's listening for my next cue. Max has been coming to the sanctuary for six weeks now, but trust doesn't come easily to him. Diagnosed with autism spectrum disorder, he struggles with sensory overload and new environments, and today he seems especially tense. *I hope he's not picking that up from me.*

"Okay, Max," I say softly, stepping up to his side. "Let's start with some deep breaths. Remember how we practiced last time?"

Max glances down at me, his expression tight. His mom stands nearby, watching with a mix of hope and anxiety.

"In through your nose," I demonstrate, taking a deep breath and letting it out slowly. "And out through your mouth. Willow's going to feel it if you relax."

Max hesitates but follows my lead, his shoulders lowering just a fraction as he exhales. Willow shifts her weight, sensing the change in his posture.

"Good job," I say, smiling. "Now let's try a little movement. We'll go slow, just a walk."

I give Willow a gentle pat and click my tongue, and she begins to move, her hooves crunching softly on the gravel. Max tenses again, his body rigid in the saddle.

"Keep breathing, Max," I remind him. "Willow's got you. She's like a big, fluffy grey pillow, remember?"

That earns the smallest twitch of a smile from him. Last week, I'd joked that Willow was softer than his favorite blanket, and he'd seemed to like that.

As Willow takes a few more steps, I notice Max's grip on the reins start to loosen. His shoulders aren't quite as hunched, and he's beginning to move with the horse's rhythm, however slightly.

"Do you want to try steering?" I ask, keeping my tone light and encouraging.

Max doesn't answer right away, but after a moment, he nods. I show him how to hold the reins just so, guiding Willow gently to the left and then to the right. He mimics my movements, tentative at first, but his confidence grows with each turn.

"You're doing it, Max!" I cheer. "Look at you—Willow's listening to you."

A small, proud smile breaks across his face, and for a moment, I see a glimmer of the confidence he's working so hard to build.

After a few laps around the ring, I stop Willow and reach one hand into my pocket for a cut piece of carrot and one of our sensory tools—a soft, colorful scarf. "Ready for a game?" I ask, holding it up.

Willow crunches the carrot while Max eyes the scarf warily. "What kind of game?"

"Let's see if you can wave this while Willow walks," I explain. "It'll help you practice balance and get used to moving your arms while you ride."

He hesitates, but eventually reaches for the scarf. I hand it to him, showing him how to hold it properly.

"Okay, just like before," I say. "Take a deep breath, and let's try a few steps."

Willow starts to walk again, and Max lifts the scarf, letting it flutter in the breeze. At first, his movements are stiff, but as he gains confidence, he starts to wave it more freely.

"Great job, Max!" I say, clapping lightly. "Willow loves how you're leading her."

Max beams, his earlier tension melting away. By the end of the session, he's steering Willow confidently and waving the scarf like a victory flag.

As I help him dismount, his mom approaches, her eyes glistening with unshed tears. "Thank you, Cammie," she says, her voice trembling. "I haven't seen him smile like that in months."

"It's all Max," I reply, glancing at him as he strokes Willow's neck. "He's the one doing the work."

Max looks up at me, his expression shy but proud. "Can I ride Willow again next time?"

"Of course," I say, my heart swelling. "She'll be waiting for you."

As I lead Willow back to the barn, I can't help but feel a deep sense of fulfillment. These moments—watching kids like Max find their confidence, their joy—is why I do this. It's not just therapy—it's a connection, a bridge to something bigger.

And for Max, today wasn't just a ride. It was a step toward trusting the world a little more.

Max's mother looks on with tears in her eyes as he reaches out to stroke the horse's mane. Max has come so far in the time I've been working with him. Nothing is more rewarding than moments just like this one.

"You're good at this," Ellis says, coming to stand beside me. His voice is softer, free of the playful edge.

"Thank you for your help with Willow earlier today," I tell him.

He glances at me, a flicker of something unspoken passing between us. "Just doing what needs to be done."

<hr>

FOR A MOMENT, I let myself relax, the weight of the day lifting slightly now that it's over. But then I hear laughter coming from the parking area out front, a light, feminine sound that sets my teeth on edge. I turn to see one of Ellis's exes, Lena, leaning against his truck, her smile radiant as she waves to him. He grins back, his posture easy, and the sight twists something deep in my chest.

"Looks like you've got company," I say, my voice cool.

Ellis follows my gaze, his expression shifting to confusion. "Lena? She's just..."

"You don't have to explain," I cut him off, turning away. "Don't forget to fill out your timesheet before you leave, for Reese's records."

I don't wait for his response. Instead, I head back to my office, the familiar ache of disappointment settling in. I should've known better than to let my guard down. People like Ellis don't change—not for someone like me, anyway.

That night, as I sit on my porch and watch the stars, I try to shake the day's events from my mind. The ranch is quiet now, the only sounds are the rustle of leaves and the distant call of an owl. But my thoughts are anything but peaceful.

Ellis had shown me a side of himself I hadn't seen before—kind, attentive, and unexpectedly patient. For a brief moment, I'd allowed myself to believe that maybe, just maybe, he could be more than the playboy everyone knows him to be.

But then Lena showing up had reminded me of the truth. Ellis McNair is a man who knows how to make women feel special, but that doesn't mean he's serious. And I *can't afford* to be anyone's passing fancy.

As the night deepens, I make a silent vow to myself: to keep my focus on the work that matters and the people who truly need me. Because no matter how patient Ellis claims to be, I can't risk letting my heart get trampled again.

CHAPTER 4

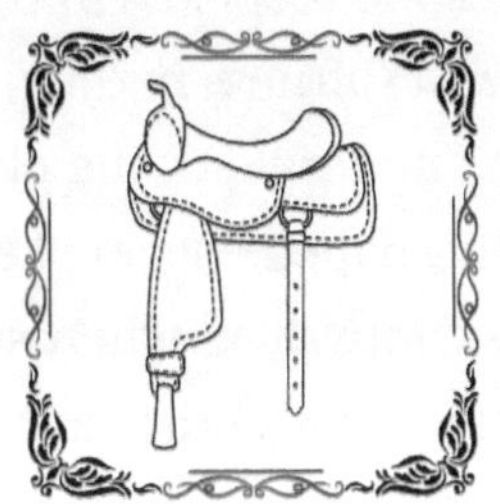

Cammie

THE LATE AFTERNOON SUN bathes Mason Ranch in golden light as I lead Honey Bee back to her stall. The mare's injury from the other day has stabilized enough for her to go on short walks around the corral. I was worried that she would regress when she was not feeling well. My intuition tells me that something else is off with this sweet girl but I can't be sure whether it is just her injury or *another cause altogether*.

I remain by her side when I can between clients. Having someone familiar is always a good idea for cases like Honey Bee. All of the horses here and the clients who rely on them are a part of my big family. I will care for all of them like relatives when they need extra support. That's just my way. And I make sure that anyone who is working around them will have the same kind of compassion for them.

My thoughts drift to the newest volunteer who seems to always be creeping into my mind more and more, recently. Ellis is over in the paddock, working to distribute a new batch of hay into the stalls. Watching him with the horses is... something.

His face is a study in strength and softness, a combination that never fails to take my breath away. His stubbled jawline is sharp and defined, giving him an air of confidence and self-assuredness that makes him impossible to ignore.

His eyes are deep and expressive, framed by neat brows that arch slightly, as if he's always on the verge of a knowing smile. Those eyes hold a quiet intensity, a focus that makes me feel like I'm the only person in the room when he looks at me. There's a softness in them too, a depth that speaks of kindness and understanding underneath the playful charm.

His lips—full and perfectly shaped—seem like they were made for smiling, though they're equally captivating when set in a serious expression. When he does smile, it lights up his entire face.

Every line and angle tells a story, and every time I look at him, I'm reminded of how much I shouldn't fall for the man behind those striking features. I shouldn't linger, but there's a pull I can't quite ignore.

"Cammie?" His voice breaks through my thoughts. I hadn't realized he noticed me standing there... *and unfortunately* staring at him.

Shaking my head, I force a small smile and step closer to the stall he's working in, resting my arms along the gate. "You're good with them," I say, nodding toward Cactus Jack who seems unperturbed by sharing his space with Ellis.

Ellis straightens, brushing hay from his hands. "I'm good with a lot of things," he replies with a smirk that's equal parts charming and infuriating.

You're his boss. He works for you. It's inappropriate. He's still friendly with his ex.

I roll my eyes, trying to keep the mood light. "Oh, I'm sure you are. But there's something different when you're with the horses. They seem to trust you." That's really saying something because these horses are the most distrusting of people. Some are better than others, but it's not unusual for a horse to become unsettled by people they don't already have a rapport with.

Ellis has helped us out in the sanctuary but not often enough that I would say he's established that rapport. Even now, Cactus Jack gives him his full attention on this task instead of panicking and putting up a fuss with a stranger near him.

He leans against the dividing wall, his cocky smirk fading into something softer. "Maybe I'm just more... myself with them. Maybe that's what makes it different."

There's a vulnerability in his voice that catches me off guard. I study him, the way his shoulders relax as he looks down at his gloved hands. "Maybe," I reply, my voice quiet.

He turns his head to look at me, his dark eyes locking onto mine. "Maybe it's you."

The words hang in the air between us, heavy with meaning. My pulse quickens to a gallop with the possible intention of what he's implying, but I don't look away. "Ellis..."

He sighs, taking a hand out of his gloves and running it over his short hair. "Look, I know I'm not exactly the guy people expect to settle down. I've got a reputation, and not all of it's wrong. But that's not all there is to me. I can want something different too—despite what others believe."

I tilt my head, curiosity and caution warring inside me. Everyone knows that he's a flirt. Though I wasn't in Alpenglow Ridge yet, people talk about how he took a right hook to the face for flirting with another man's ex-wife not even months after the divorce was finalized. It was Reese's brother, Mack, and his ex-wife is now married to someone else. But the two of them worked as hands together for years, he and Mack. Everyone one here is like family, especially the hands who spend most of their days together.

His flirtations know no bounds.

That's history at this point, but aren't we made up of all our past decisions? Rumors float around about him, especially since he hits on and takes out any beautiful woman in his path like it's his job description. And there's even more stories women have told of the great night they had with him and wouldn't mind having again.

I know that sometimes things aren't always what they seem.

Many would say unkind things about the horses I work with and the children, too.

Maybe even about me.

I'm not a judgmental person, but I want to be sure of any leeway I give this man... especially if it has anything to do with my heart.

"Then what else is there?" I ask tentatively.

He hesitates, as if weighing whether to let me in. Finally, he speaks, his voice steady though tinged with emotion. "I've screwed up a lot in the past. Relationships, mostly. I thought I could handle them, but I'd always find a way to mess things up. Maybe it's because I was too scared to commit, or maybe I just didn't think I deserved it. Either way, I ran."

I don't know what to say, so I stay quiet, letting him continue.

"When I came back here, it was supposed to be temporary. A way to clear my head and figure out what the hell I wanted, where I wanted to go. But the more time I spend here, the more it feels... right. Like I have something solid under my feet." He pauses, his gaze drifting to the horses. "Like maybe... I should stick around."

"This is your home. Your friends and family are here. That makes sense."

"It's not just that. I didn't want to stay in AR. I wanted to get out and that... didn't work out. I thought I would just kick up dust and go. Never look back. I was restless."

He shoves the glove he's holding in his pocket and the other follows the first's path. "I didn't know what to make of you at first," he admits, a small smile tugging at his lips. "You've got this fire, this way of standing your ground even when everything around you is shifting. It's... impressive."

"Impressive?" I echo, arching an eyebrow. *Has anyone called me impressive before?*

"Intimidating," he amends, chuckling softly. "But in a good way. You don't fold."

I want to trust the admiration in his voice. I want to believe that his flirting is intentional and that I won't become *one of the many*. But a part of me—maybe the part that's been hurt too many times before—can't let go of the doubt. "You say all that, but what happens when I'm no longer *impressing you*?" I ask, my voice sharp. "Will you stick around, or will you run?"

Ellis flinches, the question hitting its mark. "I don't want to run anymore, Cammie. That's why I'm telling you this. I don't have all the answers, but I'm trying. And I'm willing to try for you, if you'll let me. If you give me the chance to."

The honesty in his words is almost too much to bear. I look away knowing that flirting and all that comes with it means something entirely different to me than it does to him. So many sides to Ellis that I never knew about. Here he is being sincere and open, not a hint of the flirty teasing or patient calm...

This is something too raw and vulnerable.

I want to believe him so badly. I want to be the kind of woman who allows people in when they ask. "I don't know if I can," I admit, my voice barely above a whisper.

Ellis doesn't push. He just nods, his expression unreadable. "Fair enough."

I hurry to my office, like a coward, before he can say another word.

I FIND MYSELF IN Reese's office in the main ranch house, seeking the kind of advice only she can give.

"So, Ellis decided to bare his soul..." she says, leaning back in her chair with a knowing smile. The two of them grew up in this small town. He was a year below them in school but he's worked on her family's ranch for over a decade. I know she'll be honest with me and give me tough love if needed. *Probably with more sass than I need too.*

"Don't start," I warn, though I can't help but smile a little with her.

Reese studies me, her dark eyes thoughtful. "He's a good man, Cammie. Rough around the edges and a little more..." She taps her chin for a moment before deciding, "umm, generous with the physical affection than most, sure. But he's got a good heart in there. I know it. You just have to decide if you're willing to take the risk."

"And if I'm not?"

"Then you'll never know what could've been," she says simply. "Life is full of choices. Either you pull up your big girl panties and take that chance with him or you let it pass and never know what's there."

Her words linger long after I leave, echoing in my mind as I sit on the porch of my cabin, staring up at the stars. Ellis's confession, his willingness to open up, has shaken something loose in me.

But is it enough to make me take the leap?

For now, all I can do is sit with the question and hope the answer reveals itself in time.

CHAPTER 5

Ellis

"YOU GOT THIS," I tell myself in the rearview mirror when I pull up to the sanctuary in my truck.

I'm a few steps from my truck when I turn right back around to grab my hat from the passenger seat. I make it to the entrance of the paddock when I turn around again to grab my gloves from the center console.

I do not have this.

I'm so flustered I can't even get my shit together for my first full day shift.

Tony, the ranch manager, told me to report to the sanctuary until further notice. I couldn't have been more grateful. I'm no longer a volunteer but an employee of the Mason Sanctuary. No more splitting my time between the two.

I can focus solely on Cammie.

It's the kind of day that makes you feel alive—crisp air, the earthy scent of hay, and the distant hum of ranch life waking up. Maybe I just feel more alive because I'm here. I should be focusing on my chores and being on my best behavior, but my eyes are already drawn to her.

Looking at her, my breath catches for a moment. Her face is radiant, the kind of beauty that lingers long after you've looked away. Her skin glows. Those dark, soulful eyes of hers hold a quiet intensity, drawing me in with every glance. They seem to know every secret I've ever tried to hide. But I don't want any secrets between us or to hide that I want her.

Her lips are round and subtly glossy, with chapstick I've seen her apply a time or two, that catches the light just right—like they were made for whispering promises. Her high cheekbones add a regal structure to her face, but it's the way her cheeks lift when she smiles, that makes my chest squeeze.

There's an undeniable confidence in how she carries herself, but her expression—soft, thoughtful—reminds me that she's not just stunning; she's capable, too.

Cammie's standing by the fence, clipboard in hand, scribbling furiously like the weight of the world is balanced on that little piece of paper. She's always so damn focused, like if she works hard enough, she can fix everything.

Maybe she could fix me too...

I can't help myself. I stroll over, hands in my pockets, and lean casually against the fence. "Morning, boss. You always start the day this serious, or is it just for me?"

She glances up, her pen pausing mid-scribble. "I wouldn't have to be so serious if you weren't keeping me from working."

That gets a laugh out of me. "Me? I'm the picture of responsibility. I just wanted to check on you."

She raises an eyebrow, her lips twitching like she's fighting a smile. "Is that what you're calling it now?"

"Yep. I'll have you know I'm practically a saint," I say, crossing my arms and grinning.

She shakes her head, but I catch the corner of her mouth lifting. It's a small victory, but I'll take it. With Cammie, every genuine smile feels like earning a medal.

By mid-afternoon, the barn is buzzing with activity—or at least, it should be.

Instead, there's an unsettling quiet.

I find Cammie by Miss Ellie's stall, her face tight with worry. The mare stands unusually still, her head hanging low. Normally, Miss Ellie's full of sass, always stomping or flicking her tail. Today, she's lethargic, her eyes dull.

"What's going on?" I ask, stepping closer.

Cammie doesn't look up, her hand gently stroking Miss Ellie's neck. "Something's wrong. She's barely moved all day. And it's not just her—some of the others have been acting off too. This is the third horse who has had a stark change in behavior. I don't know what to do."

I crouch beside the stall, studying the mare. "You think it's just a bug or something? We've dealt with viruses before."

She finally meets my gaze, her expression serious. "I don't think so. I've seen sick horses, and this... isn't the same. They're sluggish, uncoordinated... like something's draining them."

Her words settle heavy in the air. I glance at Miss Ellie again, noting the way her legs tremble slightly when she shifts her weight.

"You think it's the feed?" I ask. "Or maybe something in the water?"

"I don't know," she admits, frustration creeping into her voice. "But if it's spreading, we're in trouble."

I stand, brushing hay off of my jeans. "We'll figure it out. Whatever it is, we'll handle it."

Her eyes soften just a fraction, but the tension in her shoulders doesn't ease. "I hope so," she says quietly, more to herself than to me.

The rest of the day passes in a blur of work and worry. I help her check on the other horses, taking note of their symptoms and trying to piece together a pattern. It's clear Cammie's exhausted, but she refuses to slow down. She goes into each stall and tries her best to comfort the uneasy horses or simply sit beside them as they rest in between the remaining sessions she has for the day.

"Cammie," I say as we're finishing up in the barn, "you need to take a break. You're running yourself into the ground."

She shoots me a sharp look. "I don't have time for a break, Ellis. These horses need me."

"And you won't do them any good if you collapse," I counter, my tone firm but gentle.

She opens her mouth to argue but then sighs. "I just... I can't stand not knowing what's wrong. These horses are everything to me, to the sanctuary. Without working horses we can't offer the services we do for the children. I couldn't bear it if something even worse happens to them. They're important to more than just me."

Her voice cracks slightly on the last words, and it hits me just how much this place means to her. It's not just a job or a responsibility—it's her heart.

Every glimpse I have of the deeply caring soul she is, makes me fall a little harder for her.

That evening, I find her by the corral, watching the sunset. The sky's painted in shades of orange and pink, but Cammie's not paying attention to the beauty around her. Her arms rest on the fence, her gaze distant.

"You're really worried, huh?" I ask, stepping up beside her.

She doesn't look at me, her voice quiet. "Of course, I am. These horses... they're not just animals to me. They're part of the family."

I lean against the fence, letting the silence stretch between us for a moment. Then I glance at her, deciding to take a chance. "You really think you can handle all this? I mean, nothing wrong with caring, but it's a lot to take on."

"Even if something is difficult, that doesn't mean that it's not worth the effort." There's something about the way she picks at the splintering wood of the rung that makes me think she's not just talking about the horses.

Nodding, I respond to what she didn't quite say. "I could figure out how to handle difficult things if I need to. Most are worth it."

Her lips quirk into a tired smile. "You really think you can handle me? I'm not exactly easy to keep up with."

Her attempt at deflection doesn't fool me, but I play along. "I don't want easy. Maybe once I did, but not anymore. Not for a while. And something tells me you *are* worth it."

Her cheeks flush in the fading light, and she looks away. "You're a smooth talker, Ellis. I don't buy it."

I step closer, dropping my voice. "You don't have to. But I mean it just the same."

Her brows furrow. "For what? You've got women at your disposal, clearly... Why are you even trying to convince me?"

"I'm sure you heard about the falling out Mack and I had all those years ago," I start. I don't usually bring this up. I don't think I've even talked to Taylor about it and they're my best friend. "When I woke up with a headache and a swollen face from the hits I took, I knew something had to change. It was just a thought in the back of my head for a long time. But still present. I hurt my friend, I damaged that bond. All for nothing. I don't even want Melody. Not badly enough for the consequences."

"So why do it?"

"It's... easy. I like to play around. Honestly, I hadn't even meant anything by it." I sigh. "I like to make women feel good." She grimaces. "Not *always* sexually." I huff. "There's nothing better than a smile from a beautiful woman. When it's directed at you, it's nice."

"From what I've heard, it's not just the smiles you're after." Her eyebrow kicks up on one side and I scratch the back of my head.

"What? I'm still a man. I like to have a good time, too." I shrug, debating the merits why I'm here spilling my guts to Cammie in my head. "But I want more than that. Have for a while. I want someone who will smile at me and stick around after."

"Why don't you set these people straight? You could defend yourself when people call you a—"

"Man whore?" I shrug again. "What's the point? If they have that impression of me, it says a bit more about them than it does about me. If someone truly wanted to know what I was after, then they'd ask." I make a point of meeting her gaze, putting all my intentions behind the look. She looks away under the weight of my stare.

For a moment, she's silent, her eyes fixed on the horizon. Then, softly, she says, "Why does that make me want to believe in you?"

I grin, my hand brushing the side of hers on the fence. "Maybe because deep down, you already do."

Her eyes meet mine, and for a second, I see something shift—something real. But just as quickly, she steps back, putting distance between us.

"Goodnight, Ellis," she says, her tone firm.

I watch her walk away, my chest tightening. She's still holding back, but there was something in her eyes—a flicker of hope, maybe even trust.

As the crickets start their nightly chorus, I sit by my dining room window, staring out at the darkening sky, eating dinner by myself. Between the sick horses and Cammie's walls, it feels like everything is teetering on the edge. But I've never been one to back down from a challenge.

And something tells me this one's worth every damn second.

Chapter 6

Cammie

"Alright! Announcements!" I call out in the paddock. "Let's talk about our upcoming fundraiser and some general housekeeping. Gather around..."

The sanctuary is busy today, the air buzzing with activity as we gather for the morning meeting. The sun is just high enough to cast a soft glow, and the horses' gentle nickers fill the background. I get all the announcements out of the way quickly and the group disperses to their daily work.

Ellis lingers a little longer beside me, his easy grin making the air feel lighter as I make note of the behaviors of the horses currently in the corral. He's joking about something Anna said earlier, and I can't help but laugh.

Across the way, Craig leans against the fence, arms crossed. His face is neutral, but his eyes linger on Ellis and me for a moment too long. I glance his way, catching his gaze before he quickly looks off toward the stables. He was one of the first full time ranch hands that became an employee of the sanctuary. Then Anna joined on later. I knew they had a history, but Reese assured me that there would be no weirdness with them working together.

"Alright, let's get moving," Anna says, clapping her hands toward the man next to me. She's standing close to Ellis now, teasing him about some chore he botched yesterday. He fires back with a quick retort as they walk over to the corral, the two of them laughing like old friends.

I notice Craig stiffen. His grip on the fence tightens, knuckles whitening for just a second before he pushes off and heads toward the barn without a word.

Later during a break, I'm checking on Blossom when I overhear Craig and Anna talking by the tack room. His voice carries just enough for me to catch the edge in it.

"Looks like Ellis has found himself another project," Craig says, his tone light but his words sharp. "Wonder how long this one will last."

That gives me pause. *Is he talking about me?*

Anna huffs, brushing off his comment. "Don't be ridiculous. He's just working here like us."

"Sure," Craig mutters, his voice lower now, but there's a bitterness I can't ignore.

I know eavesdropping is not right, but my mind is racing. Something about the way Craig said it wasn't just teasing. *How long this one will last* seems... ominous. There was something deeper, darker, lurking beneath the surface. Maybe there are more reasons not to trust Ellis than I thought.

<hr>

"You are so funny. Why don't you come out to the bar anymore?" A woman asks from some ways away.

The barn is quiet, save for the creak of the hayloft ropes swaying gently in the breeze. I've just finished checking on Bella, our most sensitive mare, when the sound of laughter drifts in from the front paddock. *A woman's laughter.*

My curiosity gets the better of me, again, pulling me toward the sound even though I know I shouldn't.

There he is—Ellis, leaning casually against the fence, that signature grin lighting up his face. Kendra, one of the volunteers, stands beside him, giggling at something he's said. The bubbly redhead always seemed to find excuses to linger at the sanctuary longer than necessary. And now, I guess I knew why. *She was hoping to invite Ellis out to the bar with her.*

She places her hand on his arm, and my stomach twists.

I don't need to hear the words to know what's happening. I've seen this scene play out too many times before. Ellis, charming and carefree, leaving a trail of broken hearts in his wake.

Just like I suspected.

I turn sharply, my boots crunching against the gravel as I walk away. I *don't want to see more.* I don't want to feel this... this ache that's been simmering ever since he started showing up at the sanctuary.

"Cammie!" Ellis calls out when he notices me leaving the area.

I keep walking, my jaw tight, but his footsteps close the distance between us.

"Hey, wait a second," he says, falling into stride beside me.

I whirl around, anger bubbling to the surface. "Don't bother. Just don't. I'm not going to be another one of your games."

His brow furrows, confusion flashing across his face. "Games? What are you talking about?"

"I saw you," I snap, my voice trembling despite my best effort to stay calm. "With Kendra. Flirting with her, just like you always do. Don't tell me I'm imagining it because I'm not blind." But maybe I am stupid, falling for his charm just like all those other women. *Like Kendra.*

I don't have a right to be upset. Ellis is not my–he's not *my* anything. And yet, I'm still upset.

His mouth opens, then closes. He takes his hat off, and runs a hand through his curls, the gesture both frustrated and defensive. "Cammie, it wasn't like that."

"Oh, really?" I cross my arms, narrowing my eyes. "Because it sure looked exactly like that."

He exhales sharply, shaking his head. "I was just being friendly. She was asking about the horses, and I—"

"Save it," I cut him off, my heart pounding. "I don't need an explanation, Ellis. I've seen this before. You flirt, you charm, and then you leave. I won't be another name on your list."

Something flickers in his eyes—hurt, maybe—but I don't stick around to figure it out. I turn and march into the paddock, the conversation over as far as I'm concerned. I was better off not hoping that we were making any progress.

• • • •

The ranch's vet, Kelly Lomas, arrives later in the afternoon, her face serious as she unloads her equipment. I hover nearby while she examines Miss Ellie and the other affected horses, my stomach in knots. When she was here before, she took blood samples to run some testing before this visit today. She found unusual readings for a substance in Honey Bee's system.

"Doc," I finally ask, my voice barely above a whisper, "What are we looking at here? What's causing these elevated toxin levels?"

She straightens, her expression grim. "Honestly, I don't know yet. It's not a common substance. At these levels, it's something that's being intentionally introduced—into their feed or water."

Ellis steps out from the shadows of the barn, his jaw tight. "So, you're saying someone's poisoning the horses?"

"I can't say for sure," Kelly replies, choosing her words carefully, "but it's a possibility we have to consider. We'll run more tests, but I wouldn't rule it out."

The words hang heavy in the air.

Poison.

The thought sends a chill down my spine.

I SIT ON THE edge of the horse pen, watching Bella graze under the fading light of the setting sun. Normally, this would be my favorite part of the day—the stillness, the quiet—but tonight, it feels different.

Heavier.

My thoughts drift, unbidden, to my family. Fiona and Victor, my older siblings, always seemed to have it all figured out. Fiona with her brilliant surgical career. Victor dominating courtrooms as a top corporate lawyer. And then there's me—*just Cammie*, running a non-profit therapy program in a town so small it doesn't even have its own traffic lights.

I love what I do, but it's hard not to feel like I'm always coming up short. Like I'm carving out a space for myself in a world that already has enough overachievers.

The crunch of boots on gravel pulls me from my thoughts. I don't need to look up to know it's him. I feel it with the shift in the air.

"Mind if I sit?" Ellis asks, his voice softer than usual.

I shrug, not trusting myself to speak.

He climbs onto the fence beside me, his presence warm and solid. For a long moment, neither of us says a word.

"I never meant to hurt you," he says finally, his voice low. "With Kendra earlier… I don't want you to think I'm just playing around."

I swallow hard, staring at the horizon. "Then what are you doing, Ellis?"

"I'm trying, Cammie." He exhales, running a hand over his hair. "I'm trying to figure out how to be… more. For you. For me. But I've spent so long being the guy everyone expects me to be, I don't know how to change overnight."

His words catch me off guard.

They're completely unexpected.

"I don't know if I can believe you," I reply honestly. I don't know how to be anything other than honest. I wish I could make flowery responses that don't unnerve people so but I am who I am. "Your actions say otherwise."

"I don't blame you for not believing me," he says softly. "But I'm not giving up. Not on either of us."

I want to believe that he is trying to change, but it terrifies me. It's safer to accept the conclusions I can draw from what I already know.

Falling for Ellis McNair is dangerous.

I need separation for the simple fact that you don't have to be pushed to fall.

CHAPTER 7

Ellis

CAMMIE HASN'T SPOKEN MORE than a handful of words to me in days, and each one of them is more curt than the last. The way she's been avoiding me—it's like I don't even exist anymore. I'd rather she yell at me, get angry- anything- but this cold shoulder.

I let out a heavy sigh then sip my coffee from my thermos. I could fall into old habits and chat up someone else with the weight of the silence pressing down on me from her.

But I'm not.

Even if she isn't fucking with me, I made a promise to myself that if I wanted something different from my life, then I'd have to be different. *This isn't how I wanted things to go.* When I started helping out at the sanctuary, I told myself it was just about finding my place again when I felt so lost before. That's what I told her, too. But somewhere along the way, it stopped being about finding my place back on the ranch.

It became about her.

The barn door creaks open, and I spot her at the far end, running a hand along Sundance's coat and whispering to her. She moves with the kind of grace and purpose that makes you stop and take notice. It's like she's one of them, like she was made for this life. For the first time in days, I feel like I can breathe because, at least, she looks content.

"Cammie," I call out, taking a tentative step toward her.

She doesn't look up, doesn't even flinch. It's like I've said nothing.

"Cammie, come on," I say, my voice softening. "We need to talk."

Finally, she looks at me, but her expression is guarded. Her walls are up, and I can't blame her.

"What's there to talk about, Ellis?" she says, her tone curt as it has been recently. *All business.* I like the fire she has inside. I love her quiet strength.

I just wish it wasn't directed at me like this.

I take another step closer, but she holds her ground, her gaze sharp enough to cut. "I wasn't flirting before," I say, my voice low. "I just haven't seen her in a while and we got to talking. It wasn't like that."

She snorts, shaking her head. "Somehow, I imagine it's always 'not like that' with you, isn't it? You don't even realize how much you hurt people, Ellis. Or maybe you do, and you just don't care."

"That's not fair," I snap, the frustration bubbling to the surface. "I care, Cammie. I care more than you think."

"If not Kendra, then Lena, or whoever else thinks you're down to have a *good time.* Craig told me about Anna, too. I'm surrounded by all the women you've had *relations* with," she huffs out, her voice breaking. "I don't want to talk. There's no need. *There's no point.* I'm your boss and this conversation is inappropriate anyway. We're good, get back to whatever you were working on before."

The response catches me off guard.

I don't know what Craig's problem is but I can't even be mad. I did have a thing with Anna after her and Craig split, but it was nothing serious.

And maybe that makes it worse in Cammie's eyes.

Fuck.

I don't know how to make it better or, at the very least, not make it any worse.

Telling her of every woman I've been with is not likely to win me any favor. I know it is not helping me that she's finding out about my exploits through anyone else other than me.

Fuck.

When I say nothing, she leaves for her office at the end of the hall. The door makes a definite close when she's inside and I'm firmly on the other side of it.

I SIT ALONE IN the tiny rental house I've called home since I returned. It's quiet here, too quiet, and not for the first time, it feels too empty.

Before I left, Cammie and I had both applied to live in the cabin on Mason Ranch shortly before I left town. Tony said that we could both have it when he moved in with his wife. He and Drea Montoya had basically been together for years before either of them decided to grow up and just tie the knot. We all knew they were made for each other.

When Tony offered, Cammie talked about sharing the place—just as roommates, nothing serious—but the idea terrified me. Not because I didn't want to be around her, but because I wanted it too much. I was afraid of what it would mean, afraid of what I might feel, if I let myself get too close to someone like her.

So, I did what I always do. I ran. I let her have it. I told myself I needed space, freedom.

But the truth is, I was scared.

And now, sitting here alone, I wonder if I made the biggest mistake of my life.

The next morning's black coffee goes down more bitter than the previous day as I head back to the sanctuary, determined to make things right. But when I get there, Cammie is already deep in conversation with Kelly.

"I'm telling you, Doc, something's not right," she says, her tone urgent. "Miss Ellie's toxin levels are too high to be accidental. *Someone's doing this.*"

The vet nods, her expression grim. "We'll run more tests, but you're right to be concerned. This isn't normal."

"Who would do something like this?" I ask, stepping into the conversation. She hasn't asked me to be a part of this and only reluctantly given me answers to the questions I've asked. Regardless, I'm always keeping an eye on her—just in case.

Cammie glances at me, her eyes wary. "That's what I'm trying to figure out."

Her words are sharp, tinged with worry, maybe even fear.

"Let me help," I say, meeting her gaze.

She hesitates, and for a moment, I think she's going to push me away again. But then she nods, just barely.

"Fine," she says. "But don't make me regret it."

I NOTICE CAMMIE WATCHING Anna with a suspicious look. She stands behind the partition and I join her.

"Anna's been acting strange," she murmurs to me. "She's been around the feed room a lot lately, and she's uneasy whenever I'm nearby." She turns piercing eyes on me. "I don't think it's because of the news Craig shared with me unceremoniously."

I stifle the wince, choosing to be helpful instead. "I've known her for years. She's not the kind of person who could hurt these horses." I don't add that what Anna and I had was a short thing, because it doesn't seem like it'd help me anyway. Clearing my throat, I ask, "You really think she's behind this?"

"I don't know," she admits. "But something's off."

"What did she say when you went to her?"

"She apologized for being weird. Basically saying Craig's been acting erratic lately, that she's sorry he dropped her baggage on me. He keeps bringing up the past, like it's her fault things didn't work out between them."

I follow her gaze, watching as Anna hurries across the yard, avoiding eye contact with anyone.

"I don't think we should add her to the suspect list just yet," I say, placing a hand on her shoulder. "Her and Craig dated once back when, but that's been done for a while." She stiffens at the touch but doesn't pull away. I try to lighten the mood with a joke. "I'm sure it's neither of them with so much time and energy going into their relationship problems." By the time I'm finished talking, she's relaxed slightly under my hand. It's a small thing, a step in a positive direction.

Maybe, just maybe, I can fix what I messed up.

It's now that I know for sure that I don't want the freedom. I want the commitment. I'll do what I must to earn her trust in me.

Chapter 8

Cammie

EMERIA GRIPS THE REINS, her small hands trembling slightly as Bella takes a slow, deliberate step forward. Emeria's shoulders are tense, but there's a flicker of determination in her eyes.

"You're doing great, Emeria," I say, walking beside Bella and keeping a steady hand near Emeria's knee. "Just remember to breathe. In through your nose, out through your mouth."

Emeria nods, her lips pressed together in concentration. She's working on her posture today. We've been focusing on it since she started therapy ten months ago. Diagnosed with cerebral palsy, Emeria struggles with balance and coordination, but horseback riding has given her a sense of independence slowly over the time that she's been working with me.

"Okay, Emeria," I continue, my voice calm and encouraging. "Now let's try sitting up a little taller. Imagine there's a string pulling you straight up to the sky."

Emeria adjusts her position slowly, her spine straightening as she focuses on my instructions. Bella takes another step, her hooves sinking softly into the dirt.

A little tingle of awareness rolls over me. I glance around until I meet a pair of eyes watching me. Ellis' heated gaze tracks me as I work in the corral. *It's not uncomfortable but it is heavy as a touch would be.* I give him a little nod of acknowledgment before returning to my task.

"Good," I say, smiling. "That's it. How does that feel?"

"A little wobbly," Emeria admits, her voice small but steady.

"That's okay," I reassure her. "It's all part of getting stronger. You're doing amazing!"

We pause for a moment, letting Bella come to a stop. I reach into my pocket and pull out a small textured ball, one of the sensory tools we use during sessions.

"Here's a challenge," I say, holding the ball up. "Can you take one hand off the reins and squeeze this while keeping your balance?"

Emeria hesitates, her brows furrowing. "What if I fall?"

"You won't," I promise. "I'm right here, and Bella's got you. She's the steadiest horse in the sanctuary."

Emeria glances down at Bella, then back at me. Slowly, she releases one hand from the reins and reaches for the ball. Her movements are tentative, but she manages to grab it.

"Now give it a squeeze," I encourage her. "Just like we practiced."

Emeria squeezes the ball as Bella keeps walking, her face lighting up with a mix of pride and relief. "I did it!"

"You sure did," I say, beaming. "And look at that—you're still sitting tall."

We repeat the exercise a few more times, switching hands, each success building Emeria's confidence. By the end of the session, she's smiling more freely, her earlier nervousness replaced by the air of accomplishment.

As I help her down from Bella's back, Emeria turns to me, her eyes bright. "Do you think I'll ever be able to ride by myself?"

My heart swells at her question. "I know you will," I say. "You're already stronger than you think, Emeria. Keep working hard, and you'll get there."

"Could I keep the ball?" Emeria asks, once I've helped her get situated in her wheelchair. "At least until next time."

"Sure you can," I say.

Her mother approaches, her face glowing with pride. "Thank you, Cammie," she says, her voice thick with emotion. "You have no idea what this means to us." As a non-profit, the sanctuary offers my sessions for free as long as the prospective clients meet certain criteria. For many like Emeria, these therapy sessions are a way to cut the cost of treatments that would only add another financial burden to families who can't afford another expense.

"It's for Emeria," I reply, glancing at the little girl, who's looking at Bella with love in her eyes.

As they leave, I lead Bella back toward the barn, my mind still on Emeria's progress.

There's something else lingering in the back of my mind, too.

Ellis.

His quiet presence during the session, the way he stayed in the background, but still seemed attuned to everything happening, feels different. He wasn't trying to impress me or distract me by saying something flirty. He was just... there, supporting me, my practice, in his own way.

As I brush Bella down, I can't shake the feeling that maybe, just maybe, Ellis is capable of more than I've given him credit for. Out of the corner of my eye, I notice Ellis leaning against the paddock fence, his hat tipped low, his gaze fixed on us. He's been hovering around more than usual, offering help here and there today, but I've kept my distance still.

Maybe I have been too hard on a man who doesn't deserve it.

"What is it?" I ask when he reaches me from where he was standing before.

He stops a few feet away, holding up a small box. "Brought you something. Thought it might help."

I frown, eyeing the box suspiciously. "What is it?"

"Some new sensory tools," he says, opening the box to reveal a set of brightly colored textured balls, fidget tools, and weighted wraps. "Figured they might be useful for your sessions."

I blink, caught off guard. "Where did you even get these?"

"Reese mentioned them," he says with a shrug, as if it's no big deal. "I did some research, talked to a few folks. Thought you might need some extras since I see you let the kids walk off with the ones we have here more times than not."

His voice is casual, but there's something deeper in his expression—a quiet intensity that I can't place an emotion on.

Or maybe I'm just *refusing* to place an emotion on it.

"Ellis, I…" I trail off, unsure of what to say.

"You don't have to say anything," he says quickly. "I just wanted to help."

As I watch him work alongside the horses later on, something changes in me. He's not the cocky, flirtatious Ellis I've known, but someone quieter, more grounded. He doesn't make a show of it, doesn't look over to see if I'm watching. He just works, his movements steady and deliberate.

Maybe I've been too quick to judge him.

That evening, Reese finds me sitting on the porch of the cabin, staring out at the fading sunset. In tow, she has some documentation we need to look over, as well as, some fundraiser planning ideas. I make us some tea and we get to work to finish as quickly as possible. I don't want her to miss too much time with her beautiful family back home.

"You've been quiet," she says, moving from the chair across from me at the dining table to sitting beside me instead.

I sigh, leaning back against my own chair. "It's nothing," I lie. She raises a brow at me so I sigh again. "It's Ellis. He's… confusing."

Reese chuckles. "Ellis? Confusing? Never would've guessed that."

"I'm serious," I say, nudging her with my elbow. "He's been different lately. He helped with Emeria's session today, brought me some new tools for the kids. It's like he actually cares."

"Maybe he does," Reese says simply, shrugging a shoulder.

I shake my head. "But what if it's just another game? What if I let myself believe he's changed, and then he… hasn't?"

Reese studies me for a long moment. "Cammie, I get it. Trusting someone is scary, especially someone with a history like Ellis. But people can change. Actions speak louder than words, right? So, pay attention to what he does, not just what he says and then make a decision."

I nod slowly, her words sinking in.

"Besides, he doesn't have to be *the one* to be *fun*. After Drew, you deserve fun. I'm a firm believer in social proof." She winks, "And Ellis comes highly rated."

I laugh, "You are the worst, you know that?"

"But you love me anyway!" She says, flipping her dark hair over a shoulder. "Seriously, though. Let him show you what's real and what are rumors. I know first hand that they aren't to be trusted. Alpenglow Ridge has a nasty habit of gossip. Not all of it deserves your consideration."

<hr>

THE NEXT DAY, ELLIS joins me for another therapy session. He doesn't say much, just quietly assists where needed, his presence steady and unobtrusive. At one point, Sundance gets spooked by movement in the tree line, shifting uneasily under the weight of Adam on her back. Before I can react, Ellis is there, his hand on her flank, his voice calm and reassuring.

"Easy, girl," he murmurs, his touch firm but gentle. "You're okay. Settle."

Sundance calms almost immediately, and I find myself staring at him, a lump forming in my throat. Normally, I wouldn't allow someone to be so close to my sessions. My need to have control over the situation, far too great. But, somehow I don't feel like I'm losing control when he comes to offer his help.

After the session, I sit on the edge of the corral, watching Sundance graze nearby. It's not long before Ellis crouches beside me.

He sits for several moments and thoughts of all I know about him swirl faster and faster in my mind. How honest and open he's been about his intentions and how he has apologized, even when he doesn't have to. My insecurities are my own. I can offer reciprocity to him in my own way.

"I don't know why I'm telling you this..." I begin to share hesitantly what's been on my mind today.

I'm so used to being the one who listens, being the therapist, that I forget that it's good, healthy for me to share, as well. It's a mumble but Ellis gives me his full attention.

He plops down onto the sparse grass beside me and just listens. "I've always felt... less than. My siblings—they've always had their futures planned out. Lawyer. Doctor. Making big dollars. And then there's me, working with kids and animals, trying to figure it out. Sometimes it feels like I'm just... not enough."

Ellis looks at me, his eyes steady. "You're enough, Cammie. More than enough. You've got something most people don't." I look him in the eye before he finishes. "You've got heart."

For a moment, I can't speak.

"Why are you saying that?" I ask finally, my voice barely above a whisper.

He meets my gaze, his expression earnest. When his hand brushes over mine, I don't flinch at the warmth radiating from his touch. "I'm trying to make you see that I want to know you better. I've seen a lot already and I want to see more. You'll just have to get used to that."

As the sun dips below the foothills, I realize I'm standing at a crossroads. Ellis is offering me something I never thought he could—stability, sincerity.

Am I brave enough to take it?

CHAPTER 9

Cammie

I'M TAKING MY LUNCH break by the time the sun casts long shadows over the ranch. I find Ellis leaning against what's become our spot on the fence, his hat pulled low, eyes fixed on the horizon. He's been lost in thought for a moment, so I hesitate to approach. Something about the way his shoulders slump draws me in.

After he told me that I'd have to get used to his attempts to see me better—know me better— I didn't dare hope that he was being honest. I thought for sure that I would catch him flirting with yet another beautiful woman who worked on this ranch. I didn't understand how there were so many. And also how they all seemed to find Ellis.

But he surprised me.

The quiet support was never wavering and we spent even more time together just in each other's company or he'd tell me stories about what it was like growing up in Alpenglow Ridge to fill the silence.

I wasn't much of a talker, but you learn so much from people through what they aren't saying. He told me all about his friends and his family, but never about any true meaningful romantic relationships despite having a reputation for constantly being surrounded by women. Another surprise, but this one made me sad for him.

"Hey," I say softly, stepping beside him wondering if he's thinking about that now.

He glances at me, offering a faint smile. "Hey."

We stand in silence for a while, the only sounds, the distant nickers of the horses and the rustle of the wind through the hay. It's a peaceful moment, but I can feel the tension radiating from him.

I know he was gone for a while but I never asked why. Maybe something about that has been weighing on him. "You look like you've got a lot on your mind," I finally say, breaking the quiet.

Ellis chuckles dryly, shaking his head. "You could say that."

I wait, sensing he needs the space to decide whether to share. Finally, he exhales deeply and leans back against the fence. "I've been thinking a lot, you know..." he starts, his voice low and rough. "About my fear of being tied down, fear of not living up to expectations."

I glance at him, my curiosity piqued by his blunt observation of himself. "What do you mean?"

He doesn't look at me, his gaze fixed at some point beyond us, or maybe it's in the past. "Before I came back, I was engaged. Her name was Roseangela. She was... everything I thought I wanted. Beautiful, smart, driven. We had this picture-perfect plan, or at least I thought we did."

I remember Roseangela. She's nothing like me and every bit the gorgeous woman that I would expect a man like Ellis to be with.

"She left me," he says bluntly, though the emotion is evident in his eyes. "Just weeks before the wedding. Said I wasn't what she needed. That I wasn't... what she wanted anymore. That picture-perfect plan wasn't meant to include being stuck in Alpenglow Ridge forever."

The rawness in his voice tugs deep inside me.

"I thought I'd done everything right," he goes on. "Worked hard, saved up, tried to be the man she deserved. We left for a time, but it didn't change anything in the end. It didn't matter. She walked away, and I guess I've been trying to make sure I don't allow anyone to make me feel like she did. Like what I have to offer isn't worth sticking around for."

I swallow hard, his words hitting closer to home than I'd like to admit. "I get that," I say quietly. "I'm the youngest, the one who never really fit in or measured up. They've always been so sure of themselves, and I... I guess I'm still trying to figure out where I belong."

Ellis turns to look at me, his eyes softening. "You seem pretty sure of yourself to me."

I laugh, but it's hollow. "Looks can be deceiving."

For a moment, we take each other in, the air between us thick with unspoken understanding.

"Cammie," he says, his voice gentler now, "I know there's every reason not to trust me. But being here, working with you, seeing how much you care about this place and these horses... it's made me realize something."

I raise an eyebrow, waiting for him to continue.

"I don't want the freedom anymore," he admits. "Not from this life, not from you. But I don't know if I can be the man you need me to be."

I meet his unsure gaze and give him words that I wish someone would have told me. "Ellis, you keep talking about all the reasons you can't climb this mountain," I say, my voice steady, "but sometimes the whispers are what we need to listen to, not ignore."

He looks at me, his expression unreadable. "What whispers?"

"The ones telling you it's worth the risk," I say simply. "Those loud voices telling us that we aren't enough are words just like the whispers are words. We can choose which to listen to. I had to figure that out too."

Before he can respond, the sound of hooves draws my attention. Erin approaches on Willow, calling my name. "Cammie! You need to see this," She huffs when she reaches us.

I glance at Ellis, then back at the woman. "What's going on?"

"In the feed room," she says, dismounting quickly. "You won't believe what I found."

Ellis and I follow her back to the feed room, where an unopened container sits on the counter. The label is faded, but the words "Pesticide—Toxic" are unmistakable.

"This isn't supposed to be here," I say, my stomach churning. "We don't use anything like this on the land."

Ellis picks up the container, his jaw tightening. "Who brought this in?"

"No idea," Erin says. "But it must have been tucked away behind some sacks of grain. I saw it when I was just doing the count today."

I exchange a look with Ellis, my mind racing. "We need to get this to the vet," I say. "If this is what's been poisoning the horses..."

Ellis nods, his expression grim. "And we need to find out who put it there."

As we load the container into the truck, a sense of unease settles over me.

Someone on this ranch is trying to hurt the horse, and I don't know why. I'm not sure who I can trust. But as I glance at Ellis, his face set with indignation, I realize one thing: whatever happens next, we'll figure it out together.

Chapter 10

Cammie

"THIS MAKES NO SENSE," I say to no one in particular.

My thoughts swirl like leaves caught in a restless wind. From my office window I can see the horses who are calm, grazing in the pasture. My mind is anything but. I have to figure this out so that no other horses get sick.

I need to know who is hurting these animals.

I've spent the entire day trying to piece together the mystery of the pesticide, and every road seems to lead back to Anna. But *something* about it doesn't sit right. Anna's worked here for years, and while she's been acting strange lately, I can't imagine her deliberately harming the horses.

Yet, the evidence is hard to ignore once I got the call from Kelly that the pesticide was exactly the same substance she found in the toxicology reports.

It makes no sense. Why else would the pesticide be there? Reese would never allow anything that could harm the horse to be put on the land here. Her husband, who is in charge of the decorative landscaping on the property, definitely wouldn't be using something so toxic, either.

How did it get into the feed or water?

Ugh. The more I think about it the more my mind conjures up new questions and none of them have answers.

"Cammie," Ellis's voice breaks through my thoughts. I turn to see him walking toward me, his expression a mix of concern and something deeper. I stack some papers on my desk and stand to meet him in the doorway of my office.

"What is it?" I ask, my voice sharper than I intend. I can't take any more bad news. I like my peace and I haven't been able to get any for weeks now.

He winces at my tone and stops a few feet away, shoving his hands into his pockets. He looks effectively chastised but he still admits, "I overheard you talking with Anna earlier. You still think she's behind this?"

I sigh, rubbing my temples. He walks into the office and I close the door behind him. "I don't know. I don't want to. She's been acting so... off. But I can't prove anything, and accusing her without evidence feels wrong. I don't have any other leads. These are all good people here. Either they've worked here for years or they've volunteered their free time to be here. Everyone seems *unlikely*, but it has to be *someone*."

Ellis steps closer, sitting on the edge of my desk beside me. "I get it. We can't ignore the fact that someone's doing this. Whoever it is, they're trying to hurt this ranch, and I won't let that happen."

His words are steady, resolute. There's a flicker of determination in his eyes. For a moment, we're both quiet, the weight of the situation settling between us.

"I feel like I'm failing," I admit softly, surprising even myself. "I'm supposed to be the one who fixes things, who makes it better. But I don't know how to fix this."

Ellis turns to face me fully, his eyes locking onto mine. "You're not failing, Cammie. You care more about this place and these animals than anyone I've ever met. You're trying. That's not failure. That's strength."

I swallow hard, the lump in my throat threatening to choke me. "It doesn't feel like strength. It feels like I'm barely holding it together."

He reaches out, his hand brushing against mine. It's a small gesture, but it sends a jolt through me, grounding me in a way I didn't know I needed.

"You don't have to do this alone," he says, his voice low. "I'm here, Cammie. For you. For this ranch. Whatever you need."

The sincerity in his tone is almost too much to bear. I look away, afraid he'll see the tears welling up in my eyes. "Why?"

"For you, Cammie, I'm willing to do anything," he says simply.

His words hang in the air, heavy and undeniable. I turn back to him, and before I can overthink it, I close the distance between us. Stepping between his long legs, I'm closer to him sitting on the edge of my desk.

Our lips meet in a kiss that's slow and tender, filled with all the words I haven't been able to say.

I give into the kiss and let go of all the tension that has been building in my body. Relaxing against him, Ellis holds me close.

If kissing had felt this good before, *I've never known.* I've only kissed two other men and it's *never* felt like this.

His lips move over mine as he holds my body even closer to him. Mint from his gum lingers on my taste buds, punctuating the kiss with something sweet and dizzying..

I can feel the evidence of desire he has for me pressing into my stomach. Something that I should be making a very big deal about.

If I were in my right mind, I would be making a big deal about the very hard and very large penis pressing against my body right now.

Desperation laces our movements as we take comfort from each other.

In his arms and with his lips on mine, I might be able to find my peace again.

When we pull apart, I search his eyes for doubt, for hesitation, but all I see are eyes brightly lit that make my heart ache. He truly wants me.

Badly.

This is the version of Ellis that I like best, I think to myself.

"I'm nervous about this," I whisper. Confessing my thoughts, to be just as honest as Ellis has been with me.

"Me, too," he admits, his forehead resting against mine. "But maybe it's time you stop running from it."

The moment is interrupted by the distant sound of a horse's whinny, a reminder that the world hasn't stopped spinning just because we've had this breakthrough.

"I should check on the horses," I say, stepping back, though part of me wants to stay in this moment forever.

Ellis nods, but his gaze lingers on me. "We're not done here. Not by a long shot." Promise of what more he wants to do with me in the embers of his eyes trailing my form.

He gives me a wink before adjusting himself and leaving the office behind me. I do like the idea of what his promise could mean.

As I walk toward the stalls, my heart feels lighter, even with the uncertainty still looming over us. I feel like maybe, just maybe, I don't have to carry the weight of the world on my own. Like maybe Ellis could help me see there is hope for something more even in this time of uncertainty.

I SPEND THE REST of the night updating Reese on everything I've learned and immediately she agrees with me that we should get the police involved.

This was no accident.

I don't know who did this but they can't get away with it.

It's a long night of explaining all that's happened, but knowing that the investigators are taking this matter seriously is an amazing reassurance. Mason Ranch has over sixty employees and volunteers with direct access to the sanctuary when it comes down to it. Whoever is trying to hurt the horses could easily turn their ire on any one of us. I'll suffer many more long nights if it means that I could protect any of us from harm.

CHAPTER 11

Ellis

I LEAN AGAINST THE barn door, watching the day turn into night. The horses are calm, their heads low as they graze, and for a moment, I feel the weight of the day lift.

It's peaceful out here, even when life isn't right now.

Cammie's laugh carries on the breeze, soft and easy. She's over by the paddock, her hand resting on Anna's shoulder as they chat. It's a sight I could get used to. I'm happy that her and Anna are on good terms again once all the seemingly suspicious behavior had come to light.

Anna pulled away because of personal reasons that had nothing to do with the horses or the sanctuary.

All staff and volunteers of the sanctuary have been under investigation and interviewed for the poisoning of the horses. My interview was a few days ago, but there's no telling how long it will take these cops to find anything worth something.

I hear the shuffle of boots behind me and turn to see Craig stepping out of the shadows. He's got that look again, the one I've been noticing more lately. Tight shoulders, a clenched jaw, like he's carrying something heavy.

"Evening," I say, keeping my tone light.

Ever since he told Cammie about my history with Anna, I've kept my distance, only talking to him when absolutely necessary for work. I couldn't know his motivations for trying to throw me under the bus. It doesn't take a genius to figure out why he doesn't like me though. I'm not with the drama. He can beef with him damn self for all I care.

Craig doesn't answer right away. Instead, he crosses his arms and looks past me, his gaze settling on Cammie. There's something in his eyes that makes my gut tighten—a mix of anger and frustration.

"You sure settle in quick, don't you?" he says finally, his voice low but sharp.

I frown. "What's that?"

He snorts, shaking his head. "You always do, Ellis. Ride in, flash that grin, and somehow everything just works out for you." His snide tone and what he's insinuating is pissing me off.

Seriously, what the hell did I ever do to this guy?

I straighten, my fists clenching at my sides. "What are you getting at, Craig?"

His laugh is bitter, the kind that cuts deep. "You wouldn't understand. You don't know what it's like to work your whole damn life for something, only to have it ripped away."

"Ripped away?" I echo, stepping closer. "What the hell are you talking about?"

Craig's eyes blaze as he finally looks at me. "Anna," he spits, the word heavy with pain. "She was special, Ellis. To me. And then you came along like you're hot shit and your stupid fucking smirk, and she fell for it. You broke her heart, and I couldn't fix it. And now—" He gestures toward the paddock where Cammie is still talking to Anna. "Now it's happening all over again. You don't even see it, do you? You take, and you take, and you don't care who you leave in the dust."

The words hit me like a punch to the jaw. I open my mouth to argue, to tell him he's got it all wrong, but the look on his face stops me. This isn't just anger—it's years of resentment bubbling to the surface.

"Craig, I never meant to hurt Anna. She's doing just fine," I say carefully, my voice low. "And whatever you think is going on with Cammie, it's not what you think."

Cammie and I had been careful with our stolen moments and hidden kisses. *Or so I thought.* Maybe we weren't as much of a secret as I felt we were.

He laughs again, but there's no humor in it. "Of course, it's not. Because Ellis doesn't stick around, does he? You're not even the one with skin in the game. You're just a douche, riding on someone else's land, playing cowboy while the rest of us bleed for this place."

"Wow, *I'm* the douche? For what? I'm not the one charging somebody up about their ex. You and Anna aren't together and that's not my fault." My jaw tightens. "I might not own this ranch, but I care about it. I care about the people here."

"Do you?" he snaps, stepping closer. "Because all I see is you taking what you want and leaving the rest of us to pick up the pieces."

I don't know what to say to that. For the first time, I see just how deep his bitterness runs, how much he's been holding onto.

This guy really hates me.

Before I can respond, Cammie calls my name. I turn to see her walking toward us, her smile fading as she takes in the tension between her other employee and me.

"What's going on?" she asks, her eyes flicking between the two of us.

Craig steps back, his face hardening. "Nothing," he mutters, brushing past her. "Just a friendly chat."

Cammie looks at me, her brow furrowed. "Ellis?"

I shake my head, forcing a smile I don't feel. "It's nothing," I say, even though the weight of Craig's words hangs heavy in the air.

But as I watch him walk away, I can't shake the feeling that this isn't over—not even close.

———◆•••◆———

THE WEEK PASSES WITH much of the same—working the horses, cleaning the barn, and sneaking kisses from Cammie whenever I can.

It's been nice to get closer to her. I was always looking forward to seeing her at work. But it's been better than ever since I have the privilege of touching her too.

Even if it's just a secret for now.

She is still my boss when it comes down to it. Though I don't know what Craig could have seen, we need to be careful.

I step out of the barn, wiping sweat from my brow. The atmosphere feels tense. Reese had mentioned the investigator would be back today, but she didn't say why.

Across the yard, I spot Craig by the feed shed, unloading bags of grain. His movements are jerky, his shoulders hunched as he stacks the bags up. I don't remember him being so bitter, but I suppose people change in good and bad ways.

It's midday when a black and white SUV pulls into the driveway, kicking up a cloud of dust. Two men in police uniforms get out, followed by the investigator who's been working the case. *This isn't a casual visit.* Everyone comes out of the sanctuary to see what the officers are here for.

Reese pulls up behind them in her Expedition, her face pale but resolute when she steps out. She glances at me briefly, then turns to face the approaching men.

"Craig Hagan?" the investigator calls out, his voice carrying over the yard.

Craig straightens, his back stiffening. "What's this about?" he asks, trying to sound casual, but there's an edge of panic in his voice.

The investigator steps forward, holding up a badge. "Craig Hagan, we have evidence linking you to the sabotage of this ranch, including the poisoning of the horses and financial tampering. You're under arrest."

For a moment, everyone freezes. Like a collective breath being drawn in.

Craig's face goes slack, his hands clenching and unclenching. Then, like a spring snapping, he turns and bolts toward the back fence.

"Stop him!" the investigator shouts, and the two men in uniform take off after Craig.

I don't think. My boots hit the ground hard as I sprint after him, adrenaline pumping through my veins. Craig is fast, but he's panicked, stumbling over uneven ground.

"Craig, don't make this worse!" I shout, but he doesn't slow.

One of the officers is behind me but I reach him first, tackling him to the ground. Craig struggles, kicking and cursing, but it's no use. It takes all my strength not to take a swing on him. It'd be so easy and he'd deserve every hit if he's responsible for everything.

"We've got it," the officer says behind me. The second officer helps pin him down, and within seconds, they're cuffing his hands behind his back.

"You don't understand!" Craig shouts, his voice hoarse. "This isn't my fault! I didn't mean for it to go this far!"

Reese and Cammie reach us as they get him restrained. Reese looks at him, her expression a mix of anger and betrayal. "How could you, Craig? After everything we've been through? You were family."

Craig's eyes meet hers. "I did it for the ranch," he mutters, his voice bitter. "For what it could've been. Ellis ruined everything." His gaze shifts to me, filled with resentment. "You think you're better than everyone, don't you? Taking what you want, leaving the rest of us in the dirt." He blows out a breath, literal dirt puffing away from his mouth with his position on the ground.

I step forward, my jaw tight. "This isn't about me, Craig. You nearly killed innocent animals, hurt this ranch, and betrayed the people who trusted you! That's on you." Cammie walks up behind me and places a hand on my back. It feels good to have her near me.

The investigator steps in, motioning for the officers to take Craig to the car. "We'll take him in for processing," he says, his tone firm.

As they lead Craig away, the ranch feels eerily quiet. Reese exhales shakily, her hands trembling at her sides.

"I never thought it'd be him," she whispers. "All this time, and I never saw it."

I place a hand on her shoulder, my own emotions tangled between anger and disbelief. "None of us did."

We watch as the car drives off, taking Craig—and his betrayal—with it.

His face is blank, but as they push him into the backseat of the police vehicle, his eyes dart toward the barn—and for a split second, I think I see regret.

Reese stands frozen, watching as the car disappears down the driveway. I want to say something, to comfort her, but no words feel right.

CHAPTER 12

Cammie

For the past few days, the sanctuary has been the same somber quiet with the weight of Craig being taken away. It presses down on all of us. The horses, thankfully, are recovering well, but the air is thick with unanswered questions.

I'm washing Willow in the back stall when Reese walks in, her light brown face pale instead of glowing like it usually does. Behind her, two men in button down shirts and slacks follow—one of them, Pruitt Donaldson, the investigator who's been combing through the ranch's records since Craig's arrest.

"We have confirmation," the investigator says, his voice low but firm. "Craig doctored the books and purchased the pesticide with Mason's accounts. We found the delivery receipts in his home, along with more evidence tying him to the sabotage."

Reese's mouth tightens, her lips pressing into a thin line. "I don't understand. Why would Craig do this? He's been with the ranch for years. He's part of the family."

The investigator exchanges a glance with his partner before replying. "It appears Craig harbored significant resentment toward Ellis McNair. We've pieced together his financial situation—he's been under severe strain for months. He thought sabotaging the ranch might weaken its operations enough to make you let some of the staff go and he could benefit from more hours and responsibilities. He was banking on his history with the Mason family to keep him employed. Either way he had falsified some records for time he worked for at least four months. And on a personal level... well, it seems he blamed Ellis for things that had nothing to do with the business."

Reese frowns. "What things?"

Pruitt hesitates, clearly uncomfortable. He looks over the small notepad in his hand. "It's personal, ma'am, but from what we gathered, Craig believed Ellis interfered in his relationship with Anna Varly. There's evidence in his interview and the interviews of others on the ranch that he viewed Ellis as a rival, someone who always seemed to overshadow him, whether it was in work or... affection. He had taken a liking to Cammie Clyfford and felt affronted by the closeness he observed with her and Ellis."

Reese looks stricken, her gaze flicking to me as if searching for answers. Ellis pats her shoulder and I feel the same unease curling in my stomach. She knew Craig for years. *This was a huge blow.*

"Wait," I interject, stepping forward. "Are you saying he poisoned the horses because of jealousy?"

The investigator nods grimly. "Partly. He also hoped the financial strain would push the ranch into a corner, giving him leverage. When Mason Ranch hired Ellis and added him to the payroll, that seemingly thwarted Hagan's efforts. He believed that the connection Ellis had with Cammie allowed Ellis to receive employment. It's not logical, but resentment rarely is."

My stomach churns. *Resentment.* It's such a simple word for something so destructive. All the hurt for nothing. He's lucky that the horses are recovering well or else—

"So what happens now?" Reese asks, her voice tinged with exhaustion.

"We've already taken Craig into custody," the investigator says. "We'll be forwarding all the evidence to the district attorney. From what we've uncovered, he's looking at serious charges, including animal cruelty, fraud, and tampering with property. This isn't going to go away quickly."

Reese's shoulders sag, and for a moment, she looks smaller than I've ever seen her. Her big, bold personality taking the hit because of one jerk. "I can't believe he would do this," she whispers. "He was—."

"Sometimes betrayal comes from the people closest to us," Pruitt replies, his tone gentler now. "I'm sorry this happened, but you should know—you're not at fault. None of you are."

<hr />

I FIND MYSELF STANDING outside Ellis's rental on the outskirts of town. I don't know why I came here. Maybe it's the way the day unfolded, the weight of everything that's happened, or the fact that Ellis is the only person who's made me feel steady in the chaos of the last few weeks.

I knock softly. My heart in my throat, full of yearning.

The door swings open, and there he is—shirtless, a pair of worn jeans slung low on his hips, plenty of chiseled brown skin available for my gawking. And gawking, I am.

"Cammie?" he questions, surprise evident on his face. *Happy surprise* that makes me feel a little less presumptuous for just showing up unannounced. I could've called but I just got in my car and ended up here. "What are you doing here?"

"I don't know," I admit, my voice barely above a whisper. "I just... I didn't want to be alone."

He steps aside, letting me in without another word. The condo is small but cozy, with a fire crackling in the corner and the faint smell of cedar lingering in the air.

"I'm actually glad you came," he says, closing the door behind me. "With everything that happened, it's enough to leave me a little shaken. Are *you* okay?"

I nod, my arms wrapping around myself. "It's over now, but it doesn't feel like it." Knowing that the horses are safe again makes me feel a little bit better. But knowing that I worked so closely with someone who could be so uncaring of his actions is more than unnerving.

He walks over, his gaze softening when he takes note of how I'm holding myself. "It's going to take time. For all of us."

I sit down on the edge of his couch, the exhaustion of the whole week catching up with me. "How do you do it?" I ask. "How do you keep going after everything?"

He sits beside me, close enough that our knees touch. "I don't always," he admits. "Sometimes it feels like too much. But then I think about what's worth fighting for."

His rough fingers lift my chin to meet his gaze. "Seeing you everyday, knowing I'm still building a life I want to share with the right person and being the rock that holds everything down. That's worth fighting every damn day for."

His thumb strokes my cheek and I swallow down my trepidation of the intimacy in this declaration. "I'd anchor you if you'd let me. I'd be here to support you if you needed me."

His words hang in the air, heavy with meaning. I look at him, really look at him. What I've come to love about Ellis is how open he is with me. Like just now, he had no problem sharing his heart with me.

I can share mine with him too.

Not just my heart, but my body too.

Cupping his hand with my own, I straddle his lap, enjoying the security of his strong thighs beneath me. "Do you really mean that?"

"I'm not going anywhere," he says again, his voice steady.

All the honesty.

All that vulnerability.

All of him, freely given to me.

And just like that, *I believe him.*

Time slows as my lips meet his. Like the first time, I appreciate how sweet his lips are. How gentle he's being with me.

It's like a gift of more time to experience how my surrender is totally his. I'm giving everything I can in this kiss. I'm saying yes with each soft pass of our mouths over the others'. When he nips at my bottom one, I moan into his sweet mouth.

The tension that's been building between us for weeks finally snaps, and we're tangled together, his hands in my hair, my fingers tracing the lines of his defined shoulder muscles.

There is no one around to catch us doing something we probably shouldn't. It's just us and I'm free to be his right now.

I'm holding onto him with all the strength I have. I don't want to let him go. *I couldn't if I tried.*

My hips rock slowly over his growing length. He releases my face to grab onto my hips, guiding my movements over him. Even with both of our jeans as layers between us, I can feel how turned on we both are.

My heat and his hardness.

Building and building.

When we finally break apart, I'm breathless, my forehead resting against his.

Our eyes lock again.

Leaning back, I take the tee I'm wearing over my head. My hair flops down and he smoothes it away from my face.

It is a tender gesture as I'm more exposed to him than I've been with anyone in years. The soft bra I'm wearing, doing nothing to conceal my hardening nipples.

Ellis kisses my jaw and then my neck, sending delicious tremors through me. I place my hands back on his shoulders to hold myself steady under his attention.

He skims his hands up from my hips to the small of my waist and finally at my sides. Looking up from my chest, he smirks. Unbeknownst to me, my hips are rocking again.

I want him so much and I don't care if that makes me look desperate.

I am.

"Can I?" He asks with one of his hands at the hook and eye closure of my bra.

I nod, "Yes..." and then plead, "Please touch me."

He flicks the back of the bra undone and I allow the material to fall over my arms and into his lap.

Hunger in his gaze on my chest before he weighs both of my breasts in his hands. My nipples ache, with the time he's taking to touch either one.

His head leans forward but instead of taking either needy bud into his mouth, he kisses the skin just beside it. Another kiss to the opposite side. Then a soft nip at the fullness under my nipple.

I'm beginning to believe that he doesn't, in fact, like nipples when he rolls his tongue around the tight peak.

I sigh in relief when the warm wetness of his tongue surrounds the point until he's sucking it into his mouth.

Can you come from nipple stimulation alone?

Because I'm so close that I keen like a needy little goat when his teeth graze over the sensitive skin, squeezing the other in his rough palm.

When he gets to the next nipple, I'm done for. Little sparks dance behind my eyelids with his name on my lips. I'm blissed out beyond belief as I sag into him.

Well, that answers that question.

I can, absolutely, come just from nipple stimulation.

Geez.

I hear his soft chuckle as he holds me close to his body. "I don't think I've been that close to nutting in my own boxers since I was a teenager," he admits.

If I weren't already flushed from earlier I definitely would be now. I hide my face on his shoulder.

"No, no Cammie. Baby, look at me." I don't dare look into his eyes. "That was so fucking sexy."

I scoff. "You mean embarrassing." My head still rests on his shoulder so I don't have to look at him seeing me being a mess.

He shakes his head and I feel it from how my hair moves. "No, I mean fucking sexy. I want more. I want to hear you say my name like that with you coming on me. Fuck, if I'm ever that lucky I'd have to count my blessings..."

Finally, I lean back to look at him. His cheek lifts in a smirk, "Twice."

CHAPTER 13

Cammie

I'm so wet and he hasn't even taken his jeans off yet. The material sticking to my sensitive flesh in an obscene way.

Here I stand in his living room for the first time, helping Ellis to take my jeans off. I say a little prayer of thanks that I wore at least a pair of lacy panties today.

It was not my intention this morning to be naked in front of him tonight but I have no regrets in the selection now.

He's still sitting on the couch, head dangerously close to my center. He kisses the little bow at the top of my panties and I shiver. "You look good in lace," he murmurs into my skin, just before the panties slip down my legs by his hands.

Utterly naked, he spreads my legs. Standing to kiss me, he skims over my sensitive skin with his fingertips until he finds my lips and parts them.

I'm so hot and turned on with how expertly he kisses my mouth and plays between my legs. Expertise in how he touches me so perfectly.

His fingers work me up, but I'm not coming again when he's not even naked.

I may not have done this for a while but I'm pretty sure he's supposed to be getting off too.

My hands roam over his strong body and land around his neck. *If I don't hold on, I might collapse.*

I may have wanted to hold off on coming again but he has other plans. He lays me back on the couch and puts his face between my sticky thighs. Licking up every bit of my release.

Two fingers inside me now.

It's too much and I'm dangerously close to coming despite my best efforts to hold on. It feels like I'm beyond that point of coming back to control of the pleasure sparkling up my spine.

I force my eyes open to watch him work my body so thoroughly. "Fuck you're so good at that."

His chuckle vibrates over my clit and I clench his fingers hard inside me, bringing me even closer to my edge. A few more, "Fuck, that's so good," slips out and I'm not at all self conscious about how I'm holding his head close to my body.

"I don't think I've heard you curse like that before," he says, looking up at me with dark eyes that wreck me.

"Can you blame me?" I huff, out of breath and too close to the precipice of another orgasm.

It's not fair that he's this sexy and knows exactly how to eat pussy. I *never stood a chance.* My thighs shake as I hold him in place with them. A thin sheen of sweat breaks out over me and I'm gone.

I'm here... and then I'm not, as blood rushes through my veins and I cry out his name again. His fingers keep stroking that spot inside me through the full length of my rapture. Encouraging words from his lips filter in through my consciousness.

By the time I've come down from my high, I kiss him fiercely.

A tangle of tongue and teeth, tasting myself on him has got to be the most erotic thing I've done.

He groans and I slide off the couch to kneel in front of him. These stupid jeans need to come off. *I have to see him.* I unbutton them, pausing for a moment to appreciate the sight before me.

He stands in front of me, hand cupping my chin again. "Take me out," he commands. It's a gentle command but one I'm more than willing to comply with.

Unzipping his jeans is a little difficult with how hard his dick is behind the seam, but once I do my mouth waters to taste him.

Shoving his boxers down with his pants, the full weight of him pops up, almost meeting my mouth. I take him in hand and stroke once.

He groans this guttural sound and his balls tighten. I take them into my hand and run my tongue over the head of his sizable dick. He tastes just like I'd expect when I take more of him into my mouth.

Too good to be true.

Ellis brushes my hair out of my face so that he can keep eye contact with me as he slowly feeds me more of him.

I bob over his length, our eyes never leaving each other. It's a slow pace I keep at first but the way he bites his lip as I increase the pace encourages me to go faster. "Just like that," he says. His hands on my face, helping me find the rhythm he likes, makes me throb between my thighs with need all over again.

There is no delicate way to ask at this moment but I want him inside me right now. "Condom?" I blurt.

I actually *need* him inside me and I don't want to wait any longer.

"Of course," he answers, eyes sparkling, body glistening. He picks me up and I wrap my legs around his waist as he carries me into his bedroom.

Never putting me down, we make it to the room and he grabs some condoms from the top drawer of his dresser.

My back presses to the cool wall and he rolls a condom on.

He slides into me so easily between how wet I already was and how willing I am to take him, all of him. It's a quick glide until we're joined together.

I look into his warm brown eyes and he's watching me intently. We're both panting and sweaty but there is only joy between us about crossing this line.

Each of his big hands hold me up by my cheeks. He squeezes them before asking, "Do you know how good you feel around me?"

I stifle a chuckle, "I'm confident that it feels better for me."

I attempt to move myself over his length, but he holds me in place. Looking down at where his body and mine are connected then back at his face, I'm confused on why we aren't moving closer to the orgasm I greedily want to have again.

"Cammie," he says with a pained quality to his voice.

"Ellis," I say with all the confusion I'm feeling in mine.

"I don't want this to be our last time together." A confession.

"Okay..." I respond with the same level of confusion I had before.

"This means something to me. I don't want to be with *anyone else*. I don't want *you* to be with anyone else."

"What are you saying?" I hesitate to ask in a low tone.

His eyes squeeze closed. "I don't want any more secret kisses or hiding. If we're doing this, I want it all. I want everything."

With my hand to his strong stubbled jaw, his eyes go impossibly softer when he finally meets my gaze. "I want the same. *No more hiding. No more secret kisses. We will have it all.*"

The kiss that follows my declaration takes me to a new high with him still inside me. He nips my lip and thrusts up into me. My moans and whimpers are consumed by him as he begins to push and push me right over the edge again.

The night carries on with us making our way from the wall to his bed and then his shower before I'm far too tired and sore to take him again.

Although I really want to.

He slides a steaming mug in front of me with a tea bag hanging from the side. "What's this?" I ask.

"Herbal tea or something," he shrugs. "It should be cool enough to drink now."

I sniff the mug and take a sip. My eyes widen. "How did you know I like this kind? When did you get this?" I drink more deeply from the pink rose lemon tea. It's a special blend that I have to order online because they don't stock it in the one grocery store in Alpenglow Ridge.

"I saw the little tin on your desk the other day." He must have ordered some online at some point. "I had planned on bringing some for you tomorrow morning but... you're here tonight."

This man is too much. I'm too stunned and flattered to speak.

I watch him move around his kitchen making dinner for us. In one of his t-shirts and nothing else, I should be uncomfortable. But it's nice actually.

Roast chicken breast and veggies come out of the oven smelling like actual heaven. My stomach grumbles and he's already on his way to the couch where I sit with a plate in his hand.

The food is amazing as I eat with him on the couch, my legs over his as we talk about nothing at all.

Everything looks pretty good from here.

CHAPTER 14

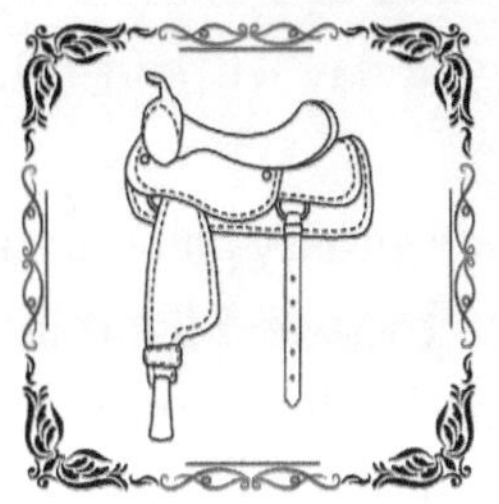

Cammie

ELLIS GLANCES BACK AT me, his cowboy hat tilted just enough to shade his eyes. "You keeping up, city girl?" he teases, a smirk playing on his lips.

I follow Ellis as he leads the way up a winding trail. Gold and amber surround us as the sun sets low in the sky. With him in front of me, it almost looks like he is the one who's glowing.

Little wildflowers bloom along the trail and sway in the light breeze around us. It's still warm from the summer sun and that little breeze feels like heaven on my skin. I let myself get lost in the beauty of this moment and Honey Bee slows a couple paces behind him. She's finally well enough to go for long rides like I suspect this one will be.

"Barely," I reply, rolling my eyes. "Some of us weren't born with spurs on our boots."

He chuckles, his deep, easy laugh echoing in the open air. "Stick with me, and you'll get the hang of it."

I might have felt defensive about his comment back when I first moved here. Though I have been riding since I was fourteen, I had never been on a working ranch before.

I met Reese years ago before she had returned here. When she found out that I had graduated and was able to practice but hadn't landed anywhere, I thought she was crazy to start a whole new organization with me.

I was eager but it was a bit of a shock moving to AR back then. Adjusting to small town life from Portland and then falling in love with the town and all its quirks. Now, I don't go a day without riding a horse to one place or another on the ranch.

The trail opens up to a wide, grassy plateau that overlooks the valley. The view is breathtaking, but it's the way Ellis reins in his horse and waits for me that holds my attention. He dismounts with practiced ease, tying his horse to a tree before turning to help me down.

"You brought me here for the view?" I ask, sliding off the saddle and landing a little unsteadily. Ells is there to help me with his hands on my hips.

"There is no better place to watch the sun set than on the foothills," he says, his voice softer now.

We sit on a weathered log near the edge of a cliff, the vastness of the landscape stretching out before us. For a while, neither of us speaks. The silence isn't uncomfortable, but it feels charged, like the moment before a storm.

Ellis breaks it first, asking, "You ever think about what you want? Like, really want? Not what other people expect of you."

I glance at him, surprised by the question. His eyes are fixed on the horizon, but there's a weight to his words that sits heavily in my chest.

"All the time," I admit, my voice quieter than I thought it'd be. "But wanting something and believing you can have it are two different things."

He turns to me, his gaze steady. "Why not? What's stopping you?"

I laugh, but it's brittle. "Where do I start? My siblings, for one. They're... everything I'm not. Successful, confident, sure of their place in the world. I've always been the one still figuring it out, the one who doesn't quite fit."

Ellis leans forward, resting his elbows on his knees. "Cammie, you've got more grit than you give yourself credit for. I've seen it. You're out here, aren't you? Sticking it out when most people would've run the other way."

His words hit harder than I expect, and I look away, my throat tight. "It's not just that," I admit, my voice faltering. "It's... Drew."

Ellis straightens, his expression shifting. "I thought your brother's name was Victor. Who's Drew?"

I nod, my hands fidgeting in my lap. "My brother's name is Victor," I explain. "Drew is my ex. We were together for three years, all throughout college. I thought he was the one. He said all the right things, made me believe in forever." I let out a bitter laugh. "Then he cheated on me with someone he met at work. I found out, he didn't even try to apologize."

Ellis doesn't say anything, but the way his jaw tightens tells me he's listening.

"That kind of thing sticks with you," I continue, my voice trembling. "It makes you second-guess everything. Makes you wonder if you're just not enough."

"You think that's on you?" Ellis's voice is low, steady, but there's an edge to it. The lines crease in his forehead and he seems genuinely ready to fight someone. Probably Drew. "That guy didn't know what he had. That's on him, not you."

I glance at him, surprised by the fierceness in his tone. "It's not that simple. It's hard to let someone in after that. Hard to believe they won't do the same thing."

Ellis shifts closer, his gaze never leaving mine. "I'm not him, Cammie. I know I've got my own baggage, but I'd never do that to you. You've got to believe that by now."

There's truth to his claims. I know that he believes that he can be that anchor for me. The guy who can hold me down.

With how I've seen him around town, I know that he has the potential to hurt me too. I don't want to fix my heart another time. Healing from Drew took time. I can't even say that I am healed because I'm still so guarded and resistant to trust anyone else with my heart.

I want to believe him.

God, I want to.

But the fear is still there, gnawing at the edges of my heart. "It's not that easy," I whisper.

"I know it's not. But I'm here, and I'm not going anywhere." He reaches for my hand, his touch warm and comforting. "But I can't stand here by myself. You've got to meet me halfway."

The moment hangs in the air, fragile and electric.

When I look at him, his eyes are steady, unwavering like they always are when he looks at me. I feel a flicker of something I thought I'd lost—hope.

The sun sinks, casting the world in a dusky glow. And as we sit there, side by side, I realize that maybe—just maybe—this cowboy might be worth the risk.

"I'm standing here with you too," I say and squeeze his hand back.

◆•◆•◆

BY THE TIME WE make it back to the sanctuary, it's dark and I'm ready to go home, shower, and sleep.

Lena is here.

She leans against Ellis's truck like the last time I saw her skulking around.

Things have changed about Ellis and me since then. We aren't hiding anymore but there is a difference in between what we were like before and after that fateful night. There's a difference between loving someone in secret and loving them in private.

Love.

Despite my best efforts, I think I do love this man.

More than that, *I trust Ellis*. He's made me trust him with his actions and how he shows up for me everyday.

"Hey, Els." Lena drawls.

I watch the two of them as she pushes off from his truck to the stables where we're putting Honey Bee and Cactus Jack up for the night.

"What's up?" He asks with a look of impatience on his face.

"A couple of us are going over to Taylor's for a bonfire and I was–"

"Gonna stop you right there. The only thing I'm doing tonight is going home with my girlfriend, making dinner and getting up to more than just sleep in bed." He winks over at me. "Is there anything else you need because you're trespassing on Mason property being here after hours like this," he says when he turns back to Lena.

She gapes at him for a moment and then glares in my direction, "Well, I—No, I don't," she huffs before stomping off to her car.

"Girlfriend?" I ask when she's out of earshot.

"Yep. Has a nice sound to it, huh?" With the sound of her tires crunching gravel out of the driveway, he winks at me, "You need help? I'm ready to get you home."

Too stunned to speak, I nod my head and he scoops me up. "Let's go," he says into my neck with a soft kiss pressed to the sensitive spot he knows will make me squirm.

CHAPTER 15

Ellis

THE RANCH IS HUMMING with the energy of a summer celebration. Mason Sanctuary is hosting a fundraiser event with a live band and catered by Reese's mom and good friend. It's small scale in comparison to the bigger events they normally put on but I think she wanted things to be more intimate. Much to my benefit.

All the staff and Reese's friends are here with their families to cheer her on in another year of success with Mason Sanctuary. Her friends are good people. Though her brother and I don't get along like we used to, everyone will be civil to keep her happy tonight. *Even Mack and me.*

This is Reese's ranch, her pride and joy, but tonight it feels like something more—a gathering place for the whole town. It's the kind of night that reminds you why you stay rooted, even when life gets tough.

Strings of fairy lights hang between the posts of the massive backyard behind the main ranch house. Their warm glow, casting a warm hue over the crowd. Long wooden tables are set up under the open sky, laden food. Reese's mom, Chandie, makes the best barbecue and she's used to feeding an army of people, AKA all us hands. There's trays of smoked brisket and ribs along with my favorite corn on the cob and plenty of other sides.

There's even pies in every flavor imaginable from Drip and Whip, the local bakery owned by Reese's friend, Drea Montoya. Kids dart between the tables, their laughter ringing out like music, while singing and acoustic guitar spills from the makeshift stage near the house. One of our own local celebrities, Tyson Abrams, plays with his band as his wife sits on the edge of the stage with only eyes for him.

Cammie and I talk with other guests as the party takes place. She's been in Alpenglow Ridge long enough for people to recognize her and have their own anecdotes to share about and with me. With my arm around her shoulders, I smile at the way the people of my town have received her and how her heart has touched so many here. *I'm not the only one that saw past her prickly, cold shell.* A few of the patients she works with are here with their families. I spot Max and Emeria talking with some of Reese's kids over by the bonfire.

"Do you want another drink?" I ask her when I notice my beer has gotten low.

"Please," she says. "And a slice of that yummy-looking cherry pie." Her smile is soft and I relish it. Gone are the soft, small smiles from before. This one is broad and relaxed with wrinkles at the corners.

I glance around, taking it all in.

I'm actually not going to the coolers to get us more beers or to the dessert table to get pie.

My eyes keep drifting to wherever she is as she mingles about.

Cammie stands near the dessert table now, clearly impatient when it comes to cherry pie, talking with Reese and Drea about the dessert. Her sage green dress flows around her legs like water, and her distinct laughter carries over the crowd to me, light and sweet. She doesn't see me watching, and for a moment, I let myself just look at her.

She's why I'm doing this.

I tug at the collar of my shirt, feeling the weight of what I'm about to do settle over me. Public declarations aren't exactly my style. I'm usually a *let's keep it between us* kind of guy. But, if there's one thing I've learned about Cammie, it's that she deserves more than quiet words in the dark.

She deserves the kind of love that you don't hide, the kind that stands tall for everyone to see.

Reese catches my eye from across the yard and gives me a subtle nod. The music fades, and the chatter around the tables starts to quiet as people realize something's happening. I step up onto the small stage, the wooden planks creaking under my boots, and grab the mic Tyson hands me with a muttered, "Thanks."

"Evenin', everyone," I start, my voice steady despite the nerves twisting in my gut. "First off, congrats on another year Mason Sanctuary. It's good to see so many familiar faces, and even better to see this place thriving the way it deserves to after the mess we had here earlier this season."

A murmur of agreement ripples through the crowd, and I take a breath, my eyes finding Cammie again. She watches me with curiosity, slowly making her way over to where I stand.

"But there's another reason I wanted to get up here tonight," I say, my voice lowering. "Something I've been wanting to say for a while now."

The crowd quiets even more, and all I can hear is the hum from the speaker beside me and the thudding of my own heart.

"Cammie," I say, my gaze locking onto hers. She freezes, her eyes wide as the spotlight of the moment lands squarely on her.

"I don't know if you realize it, but you've changed me," I continue, my voice growing steadier. "When you showed up here, I thought you were just passing through, just another city girl who'd take one look at ranch life and run the other way. But you stayed. You stayed, and you worked harder than anyone expected, including me. And somewhere along the way, you did something I wasn't ready for. You made me want more."

The crowd is utterly silent now, every pair of eyes bouncing between me and Cammie. She's staring at me like she doesn't quite believe what she's hearing, her hands clutched together in front of her.

"I've been a fool more times than I can count," I admit, my voice softening. "But if there's one thing I'm sure of, it's you. I'm done running from what I feel. So here I am, laying it all out in front of everyone. Cammie, I'm falling for you, and I'm not afraid to say it." I spread my arms wide out beside me, shouting the words without the mic, "I love you, Cameron Clyfford!"

The words hang in the air, heavy and electric. For a second, she doesn't move, and I swear my heart stops. Then, slowly, she steps forward, weaving through the crowd until she's standing right in front of the stage.

"Ellis," she says, her voice trembling just enough to make my chest ache. "You don't play fair, you know that?"

A ripple of laughter runs through the crowd, but all I can see is her. My palms sweat with my nerves as I wait for her response. "Well?" I ask, leaning down toward her, my voice dropping low. "Did it work?"

Her lips curve into a smile, soft and unsure but real. "Maybe," she whispers.

That's all I need.

I jump down from the stage, closing the distance between us in a few quick strides. The crowd erupts into cheers as I pull her into my arms, but their noise fades to nothing the moment her lips meet mine.

It's not a kiss for show—it's real, raw, and full of everything we've been holding back. When we pull apart, her cheeks are lifted with her smile, and her eyes shine with something that looks a lot like faith.

Faith in me.

Faith in us.

"You're incorrigible," she murmurs, but there's no heat in her words.

"And you're into it," I reply, my voice dropping low to whisper in her ear. My words only for her.

"I love you, too, Ellis McNair."

The crowd cheers again, but this time I don't care who's watching. I press my lips to hers in a kiss that burns like fire through my soul at her acceptance of my love.

Cammie's in my arms and she's all mine.

We barely make it to my truck, with how hungry I am for her. The drive to the sanctuary is short. I don't think I could make it all the way back to my place or hers on the opposite side of the ranch.

Neither can she.

Her hands are already creeping up my shirt when we get to the parking lot. Fingertips rolling over my stomach and into the waistband of my jeans.

She takes her favorite seat, my lap. Her dress already up and over her hips.

"No one has ever made such a big deal about loving me before..." She kisses my neck. "What else will you make a big deal about?" Another kiss to the other side of my jaw.

She's ready and I can already feel the heat coming off her sweet center.

"Everything. I *told you*. I'll make an announcement every time you make me nut if I thought I wouldn't get fired for all we've done on that desk." Her head falls back with laughter and I take that moment to run my hands over her body.

She's not wearing any panties and I maneuver her onto the bench seat. "Baby, you're really teasing me here. Is that pussy wet? Let me slide in."

"Find out," she says, wrapping her legs around me and pulling me into her body. I make quick work of pulling my dick out and putting a condom on from my wallet.

I've learned to never be caught without one when it comes to Cammie. She drives me crazy.

We both let out a breath when I'm finally deep inside her, pelvis to pelvis as I lean over her. I take as much time as I can to kiss all the exposed skin available to me and nip at her stiff little nipples still covered by her dress.

She reaches back to open a window so it doesn't get too steamy in here and I love how she thinks of everything.

"Ellis, please," she begs and writhes under me. I love to tease her and make her desperate for my dick. Once, I had told her that patience was one of my virtues. I'll give her what she wants but only after I've gotten her to her breaking point.

I slide the straps of her dress over her shoulders, kissing every inch of her smooth brown skin. She shivers and moans, her hands running over my back and back to my curls. She tugs at my short hair but I don't rush my assault of kisses until I get to her pretty little nipples. She's so sensitive there that it barely takes anything to make her come.

Her pussy grips me tight when I take the peak between my teeth, sliding the sharp edge over her sensitive skin.

She cries out and her tight core flutters over my dick. Her little feet locking behind my back to keep me close inside her.

It's my name on her lips, "Ellis, god damn. Ellis, please. Fuck oh my god."

It's only *me* who makes her scream and curse like this in the parking lot outside of her place of work.

I love this woman beneath me. Cammie is the one I was looking for and I can't believe I found her.

I let go and let her have everything I have to give. Every stroke and every thrust because I know she deserves an orgasm but so much more too.

And I'll be the one to give it to her.

CHAPTER 16

Cammie

"ALL RIGHT, CAMMIE," HE says, tipping his hat back. Ellis stands beside me, his hands on his hips, surveying the field like he's scouting for cattle. "The best pumpkin is out there, and we're not leaving until we find it."

The pumpkin patch on the Saunders' land sprawls out before us, a sea of orange under the crisp blue sky. Kids playing in the rows of pumpkins, their laughter carried on the autumn breeze, while families pose for pictures by the hay bales and scarecrows. The air smells of cinnamon, apples, and woodsmoke, and I can't help but feel a little giddy.

I arch an eyebrow at him. "Best pumpkin? What does that even mean? They're probably all fine."

"It *means* we need one that's big, round, and—" He pauses dramatically. "Not lopsided."

I laugh, nudging him with my shoulder. "Didn't you just tell me lopsided pumpkins have character?"

"Sure, but this is a competition," he says, grabbing a wheelbarrow and gesturing for me to follow him down an emptier row.

"A competition?" I echo, trailing behind him as I wonder how big a pumpkin he plans on getting that would require a wheelbarrow.

Also, where in the hell did he get a wheelbarrow?

"Yep. Winner gets bragging rights." He grins straight white teeth at me over his shoulder, his brown eyes sparkling with mischief. "And maybe a slice of that pie you keep talking about."

"High stakes," I tease, scanning the rows. I'd do just about anything for a slice of pie from Drip and Whip. "All right, cowboy. You're on."

We wander through the patch, Ellis inspecting each pumpkin with exaggerated seriousness. At one point, he crouches down to examine a particularly small one, turning it this way and that before holding it up like a trophy.

"This one," he declares, his voice solemn. "This is the one."

I burst out laughing, the cackle coming deep from my belly. "Ellis, that's the size of a grapefruit! Can we even call that a pumpkin? It's not ready, still a baby."

"Exactly," he says, carefully placing the palm sized gourd into the wheelbarrow. "It's compact. Efficient. The future of pumpkins."

"You're ridiculous," I say, shaking my head.

"Ridiculous and winning," he counters, flashing me a smug smile.

Eventually, I find a pumpkin that meets his criteria—big, round, and only slightly lopsided. We haul it back to the cabin at the ranch. The cabin we both live in now, like I suggested all that time ago.

This time, we're not at all *just roommates*. There aren't any rules that say he and I can't date because I'm his boss. Besides, I think everyone kind of got the hint that there was something going on between us when he yelled about how he loved me at the fundraiser a few months back.

Ellis insists on carving his tiny pumpkin immediately, and I can't say no, especially when he drags out a stack of carving tools and a playlist of country songs to set the mood.

We spread newspapers over the kitchen table, and soon the kitchen is filled with the sound of scraping and our laughter.

Ellis's attempt at carving a cowboy hat onto his pumpkin goes horribly wrong, leaving it looking more like a deflated mushroom. *He should not quit his day job and go into this professionally.*

"You're not allowed to judge," he says, pointing his carving tool at me as I stifle a laugh. "I know all your looks and that one is judge-y."

"I'm not judging," I say, grinning. "I'm admiring your... creative vision."

"Uh-huh." He narrows his eyes at me, then gestures to my pumpkin. "And what's your masterpiece supposed to be?"

I glance at my pumpkin, which has a crooked smile and uneven eyes. "A pumpkin with character," I say, smugly.

He snorts, shaking his head. "Touché."

When we're finally done, we step back to admire our handiwork. Our pumpkins sit side by side on the table, their carved sides flickering in the light of the candles we've placed inside.

"They're perfect," I say softly, leaning against him. He turns his head to look into my eyes and give me the sweetest kiss.

"Not bad for a day's work," he agrees, his arm sliding around my shoulders.

We stand there for a while, the smell of pumpkin and pie filling the air, and I can't help but think that this—this moment of simple, unfiltered happiness—is something I'll remember for the rest of my life.

***

THE SKI LODGE SMELLS of pine fills the air as we lace up our boots. Took us a few hours to get here but it's our first real trip together out of Alpenglow Ridge. Outside, snow blankets the world in white, the slopes alive with skiers gliding down the mountain. I can see my breath in the cold air, and even though I'm bundled up, I can still feel the bite of winter on my cheeks.

Ellis is by the lift, waiting with his board tucked under his arm. He looks ridiculously good in his jacket and hat, the kind of guy who seems to belong on the cover of some outdoorsy magazine. It never fails to amaze me how sexy this man is no matter what he's wearing. When he catches me staring, he smirks and winks.

"You ready, or are you backing out?" he teases, raising an eyebrow.

I roll my eyes. "You act like this is my first time skiing."

"I don't know, Cammie," he says, falling into step beside me as we head toward the lift. "You talk a big game, but let's see if you can keep up."

"Please, it'll be you who's in my powder," I shoot back, trying to ignore the flutter in my stomach.

The lift ride is quiet, the two of us suspended in the stillness of the mountain. Snowflakes drift lazily around us, catching in the fur on my hood and melting against my gloves. Ellis doesn't say much, but every now and then, I catch him glancing at me, his expression soft.

When we reach the top, I take a deep breath, the expanse of the slope stretching out before us. It's beautiful, the snow sparkling like diamonds in the sunlight.

"Ready?" Ellis asks, strapping his boots into his board.

"Born ready," I reply, adjusting my goggles.

He takes off first, carving smooth, confident lines down the mountain. I follow, the rush of the wind in my ears and the thrill of the speed making me forget everything else. For a while, it's just us and the mountain, the world a blur of white and blue.

At the bottom, Ellis waits for me, his cheeks ruddy from the cold and his grin wide. "Not bad, Cammie," he says as I come to a stop beside him.

"Not bad?" I repeat, laughing. "I crushed it!"

He chuckles, brushing a stray snowflake on my face when I take my goggles off. "Okay, fine. You were amazing."

The rest of the day passes in laughter and competition. We race each other down the slopes, take goofy pictures in front of the lodge's giant snowman, and warm up with cups of spiked hot cocoa by the outdoor fire pit.

As the sun begins to set, painting the sky in shades of pink and orange, we decide to take one last run. The mountain is quieter now, the slopes bathed in the soft glow of twilight.

Ellis and I pause at the top, taking in the view. The town below twinkles with lights, and the mountains in the distance look like something out of a postcard.

"It's beautiful," I say softly.

"Yeah," he agrees, but when I glance at him, he's looking at me instead of the view.

My cheeks heat, and I look away, pretending to adjust my gloves. "You're such a sap."

"Maybe," he says, his voice low. "But it's hard not to be when I'm with you."

Before I can respond, he takes off down the slope, his laughter echoing in the crisp air. I follow, my heart alight with joy.

When we reach the bottom, Ellis pulls me into a hug, spinning me around as snowflakes swirl around us. I can't stop laughing, the sound mixing with his as we stumble into the snow. Cold lips warming on each other.

In that moment, with the world wrapped in winter's magic and his arms around me, I know I'm exactly where I'm meant to be.

***

SPRING ARRIVES IN A burst of color, the ranch sparkles with blooming wild-flowers and the promise of new beginnings. One warm evening, as the sun dips low on the horizon, Ellis texts me to meet him at the old ash tree at the edge of the pasture.

The air smells of fresh grass and blossoms as I walk toward him, my heart fluttering with anticipation. He's waiting by the tree, the golden light casting him in a way that makes my breath catch. He always looks good at sunset.

"Cammie," he says as I approach, his voice steady and warm, "you've made this place—my life—something I never thought it could be again. You've made it home."

I blink, my pulse quickening as he steps closer, reaching for my hands.

"I've been thinking about this for a while now," he continues, his brown eyes never leaving mine. "You and me—we've got something real, some-thing worth holding on to. And I don't want to spend another day without making sure you know just how much you mean to me."

He pulls a small velvet box from his pocket, dropping to one knee with a confidence that radiates from him. "Cammie," he says, his voice thick with emotion, "I don't have a lot to offer—just my heart, my loyalty, and a promise to love you every day for the rest of my life and I hope that's enough. Would you be my wife?"

The tears come before I can stop them, spilling over as I nod. "Yes, it's more than enough," I whisper, then louder, "Yes, Ellis, I'll marry you."

The grin that breaks across his face is pure joy, and then he slips the ring onto my finger—a delicate gold band with a small oval diamond flanked by two tiny sapphires, one on each side. It's perfect—understated yet full of meaning, like the life Ellis and I are building together. It feels like the final piece of a puzzle falling into place.

He stands, pulling me into his arms, and our kiss is filled with everything we've been building—love, trust, and the promise of a future together.

As we sit beneath the oak tree, watching the sun dip below the horizon, I lean against him, my head on his shoulder. The doubts and fears that once held me back feel distant, replaced by something steady and true.

Hope.

With Ellis by my side, I know we're ready to face whatever comes next. *Together.*

CHAPTER 17

Epilogue - Cammie

IN THE FOLLOWING SPRING, the morning of my wedding day, the big event tent has been transformed into a rustic dream, draped in white linens and twinkling lights, with mason jars full of daisies and lavender lining the aisle. Reese's husband, Cory, helped design the concept for all the arrangements and bouquets. I'm so grateful because I don't know the first thing about flowers and the like. He nailed my vision, even with my limited direction. It's simple and beautiful, exactly what I'd hoped for.

I stand in the small bridal tent, adjusting the lace on my dress and trying to calm the butterflies in my stomach. The floor length slip dress is covered by fine lace that adds a bit more modesty with the long sleeves and high neck. It still hugs my curves and I know Ellis will have a good time teasing me as he undoes all the little buttons at my back. My hand instinctively brushes against my engagement ring. I've taken up a habit of doing so whenever I think of my fiancé.

My mom steps into the tent, her smile warm and her eyes misty. "You look beautiful, Cameron," she says, her voice thick with emotion.

"Thanks, Mom," I whisper, my throat tightening.

Having my family here means everything. My parents and siblings flew in a few days ago, and though we've had our differences in the past, their presence feels like a bridge being rebuilt. Last night at the rehearsal dinner, my dad pulled me aside and told me how proud he was of the life I've created here. It was the first time I've ever felt like he truly saw me for who I am, not who he expected me to be.

"How's Dad holding up?" I ask her, smiling through my nerves.

Mom chuckles. "He's outside, pacing like he's the one about to get married."

That makes me laugh too, and the sound feels good—light and free.

Meeting Ellis's family a few months ago was a completely different experience. They welcomed me with open arms, his mom pulling me into a hug before I even had a chance to say hello. His brothers teased him mercilessly about how smitten he is, but their affection for him—and now for me—was clear. Knowing that I already have a place in their hearts gives me a sense of belonging I didn't realize I was craving.

"Cammie?" Reese pokes her head in, her smile wide. "It's time."

I nod, taking a deep breath as she hands me my bouquet of wildflowers. My heart races, but it's steady too, like it knows this is where I'm meant to be.

The music starts—a soft, acoustic guitar melody that fills the air—and I step out. The guests turn to look, their smiles warm and welcoming, but I only have eyes for one person.

Ellis stands at the end of the aisle, looking as unfairly handsome as ever in his tailored suit and tie. His hat is tucked under his arm. His dark hair is taper cut and lined up to perfection. His eyes are locked on me.

Just Cammie.

I can see the emotions flickering across his face—love, pride, a touch of awe—and it's enough to make my steps falter for a moment.

But then he smiles, that lopsided grin that makes my heart flip, and I find my strength again.

The ceremony is quick and sweet, exactly how I want it. Anna hands me the rings with a wink, and even the horses seem to watch quietly from their pasture, as if they know this is something special.

When Ellis takes my hands in his, the rest of the world fades away. His voice is steady as he speaks his vows, each word hitting me like a promise carved in stone.

"I didn't know I was looking for you, Cammie," he says, his voice low and carrying. "But you found me anyway. You've made me better, stronger, and braver than I ever thought I could be. I promise to stand by you, to love you, and to keep running toward this happiness with you, no matter what."

My voice shakes as I speak my vows, but the words feel like they've been in my heart forever. "Ellis, you've shown me that love doesn't have to hurt. That trust is something you build, brick by brick, and that it's worth fighting for. I promise to love you fiercely, to stand with you, and to always believe in us."

When the officiant pronounces us husband and wife, Ellis pulls me into his arms, his kiss sealing the moment with all the love and passion we've found together. The guests cheer and the horses neigh in the background. *I feel like I've found my home.*

The reception is a joyful one—dancing under the stars, the clink of glasses during toasts, and the laughter of friends and family echoing through the night. Reese's speech has everyone in stitches, and Anna's heartfelt words bring tears to my eyes. Ellis's friend Taylor even has a speech that makes our family awe as they recount their friendship through the years. I'm so grateful to have them in our lives.

As the evening winds down, Ellis and I sneak away to the quiet sanctuary with the horses as our refuge. He wraps his arms around me as we lean against the fence, watching the moonlight dance on the fields.

"You're my forever, Cammie," he says, his voice soft and full of promise.

"And you're mine," I whisper, leaning into him.

The sanctuary feels alive, a place of healing and hope, just like us. As we stand there, the stars above us and the world stretched out before us, I know this is only the beginning.

And I can't wait to see what comes next.

THE END

Thank You for Reading!

Thank you for joining me on this journey through Hope by the Horizon. Your time and support mean the world to me, and I hope you've fallen in love with the characters and their story as much as I have!

Share Your Thoughts

If you enjoyed this book, leaving a review is one of the best ways to support authors like me. Reviews help other readers discover stories they'll love, and your voice matters! **Leave your review on Amazon or your favorite review site!**

Keep the Love Going

Saddled with Finesse: Can their unexpected kiss ignite a love strong enough to overcome the shadows of her past and give him the fresh start he's been searching for?
Tropes: Returning to hometown, Single Dad, City Boy/Country Girl, He Falls First, Close Proximity

Whisk til Peaked: Trapped by a snowstorm in a luxury resort with only one bed, a single mom and her loyal best friend must confront unspoken desires and buried secrets that could shatter everything they hold dear—or finally bring them together.
Tropes: Best Friends to Lovers, Single Mom, Snowed in/Forced Proximity, He Falls First

You can find all my books on my website: www.zeakayleighgalan.com

Stay Connected

Want to be the first to hear about new releases, exclusive content, and special offers?
Sign up for my newsletter at www.zeakayleighgalan.com/news

A Special Treat Just for You

Keep reading for the first chapters of Saddled with Finesse, the first book in the Alpenglow Ridge series.
Thank you for being part of this journey. I can't wait to hear what you think!
   With love and gratitude,
Zea Kayleigh Galan

Saddled with Finesse

Chapter 1 - Reese

TEDDY : IT'S BEEN A while.

Cold sweat collects down my back. Holding the phone with both hands, I lean onto the serving station. My elbows sting against the grooves of the rubber tray beneath them. This table's bar drinks are currently sweating and getting watery.

"You gonna run these or what?" My manager, Jamie, snaps me out of my state of panic.

A *while.*

Nine months is more than a while. And if I have any say in it—which I do—to say I never want to see Teddy again is an understatement.

"Relax, Jamie! I'm going." I slide the phone into the middle pocket of my standard Peak's Restaurant apron. Each drink gets placed strategically on my tray so that I can carry them all to my awaiting table. The last thing I need is to be doused with whiskey, coke and beer tonight.

Oh how the bougie have fallen.

In the time it takes to walk these drinks over, my mind has begun to wonder about the text. Why is he messaging me now? I've stayed out of his life. Asked for nothing. I've said nothing to anyone. I've been good.

Why now?

After I place the drinks on the table, I go into my spiel about the specials for dinner today. Twirling a bit of my blonde ponytail around my finger as I pop my gum. Peak's isn't known for its culinary prowess. *Mostly* men come to this place for the beautiful women in tiny, tight tops and shorts. I knew that and *they* know that. Given this information, it also does not shock me that I'll be carrying nearly one hundred and fifty fried chicken wings back to this table... accompanied by an equal amount of fries.

I read back the order to them, "Six Quarter baskets with extra crispy fries, extra ranch, coming up!" I look back to my notepad, "Scratch that, one with extra blue cheese." The man sitting in the far corner winks at me.

I'm used to how these guests treat us, at this point. They think that because I'm in this skimpy uniform I might give them a happy ending with their fried chicken.

This isn't a strip club and I'm no dancer.

Somehow talking about blue cheese has elicited this skeevy wink. *Gross.*

Tips are the reason I'm here though. I just smirk briefly before turning on a heel to enter the order in for the kitchen.

Better for them to think they have a chance... before the bill comes out.

The night drones on this way as the dinner rush picks up and I get into a rhythm of constant movement. Bouncing from table to bar, to putting in another order with the kitchen, to table to bar to putting...

You get it.

I'm thankful for the influx of guests. It means I can keep my thoughts off of the phone currently burning a hole in my apron. Every time I thought I had a second to check a notification, I would get a new table before I could even unlock the screen.

I couldn't check, but that didn't mean my mind wasn't going over every possible reason why *he* would send that message. The last time I saw him face to face, I was wiping blood from the corner of my mouth.

Never again.

My sidework to close out my shift flies by with my mind spinning over what sparked his message. Marie and Karla don't mind filling in my silence with talk about how their tables drove them crazy tonight. I nod at the appropriate times and walk out to my car with them after we lock up for the night.

Driving in the silence of my Mustang and trudging up the three flights of stairs all blur with how exhausted I am. I have no plans to move from my bed until the sun comes up.

Thanks to my infatuation with Teddy, a man who was never any good for me, I'm living in Denver. I like it here, but it's not home.

I toe off my work-mandated, slip-proof black sneakers at the door of my tiny studio apartment. Promptly flopping face-first onto my bed, drained from how busy the night was.

The stack of cash from the tables I served tonight goes into the jar I have under my nightstand. Thankfully, I can reach it from where I lay sprawled on the bed. Sliding the apron from under my body, it thunks to the carpet. I had completely forgotten my phone was in there. I'd been on autopilot the whole way home.

With a huff, I scooch my body close enough to the edge of my bed using as little energy as possible to retrieve my phone. I could use some mindless scrolling until I pass out.

My social media was once glitz and glamour. Pictures of me at this five-star restaurant. Pictures from this fancy trip wearing the shoes everyone was salivating over, but could never afford. Selfies of my flawless beat at the dinner party only six-figure men could afford to attend. Everyone in my hometown thought I was living a charmed life because I did my best to show it that way. Leaving out all the darkness behind the scenes.

Now, I barely post anything outside of the occasional thirst trap.

What?

I'm still fine as hell. Just broke.

Likes and comments from a post I shared earlier today line up neatly down my screen. It was an old picture of me at the ranch surrounded by the staff and my parents. The horses moseying about in the background of the photo twist my heart in knots. The last day I was in Alpenglow Ridge. Maybe the last day I was truly happy.

Teddy : I want to see you. Are you home?

Home?

My tired brain finally makes the connection. I hardly ever post about my past. It's too painful and unattainable after everything I've done. But, I felt homesick this morning.

I missed my family.

I missed my friends.

All the people in this photo mean so much to me and I barely get to see them now. The last time I did was when my father was recovering in the hospital after a massive heart attack. With tearful eyes, I gave and received hugs from every one of them who came to visit.

This picture had been the last we'd all taken before my father's health took a plunge. Like the shitty daughter I am, I left before the lies I told could catch up to me.

That was six months ago.

I don't respond to his text. There is nothing to say. I clear the notifications with a flourish. Reaching blindly for my charging cable, I plug my phone up to charge and slide it onto the nightstand. Wrapping the comforter around my body like a burrito, I give into the drooping of my eyelids. I let my exhaustion overtake me.

***

My ringtone blares into the small space, waking me with a start. Pawing the general area of the nightstand to find my phone is not as effective as I'd like it to be. I hear it thunk to the ground. *Great.* Fully awake and frustrated now, I kick with ferocity at the blanket to free myself.

At least, the sun is up.

I don't check to see who's calling before I answer the phone. "Good morning, honey! Did I wake you?"

"Mom, you know you did. I work nights." I try to keep the eyeroll I'm doing out of the tone of my voice, but she knows me better than that.

"Well, we're on ranch time here so I've been up for a couple of hours. You do remember what time we get started right?" The playful teasing in her tone makes my heart squeeze a little too tightly. I rub at my chest.

Sighing, I respond, "Yea, I remember." Looking at my phone to see if there were any texts I missed from her before I picked up the phone, I ask, "Is dad alright?"

"Oh yes! I didn't mean to alarm you. Or maybe I did... since this was a wake-up call." She chuckles at her own joke. "It's nothing that dreadful, thank God. Your daddy wants to talk."

"And you're sure it's to me?" My huff is long. I love my dad, but my refusal to work at the ranch is a major point of contention for us. When I left, I didn't give any reasoning or time for him to adjust to the abrupt decision I had made. The opportunity for more came to me and I did everything I could to take advantage of that as quickly as possible. I had always felt that the things that cost at least a comma and, or, have some sparkle were what my life should consist of. Ranch life though, doesn't come with the same razzle-dazzle I was after.

With his heart, I hate being the focus of his attention and causing him more stress. My choice is the same. It makes me feel twice as bad for letting him down.

"Yes, Riesling. Your dad is being cryptic with me and I can't stand it. I tried to use a little back rub to get him to give me any sort of details. I barely got this irritating task of trying to get my only daughter to come home for once."

I was there last month to get my hair done. There for the appointment and left shortly after, but I was there, technically. I just didn't see them.

"Okay... Please don't ever share about you and dad rubbing anything with me. It's... strange. Definitely too much information at—" I pull the phone from my ear to check the time. "—eight AM on a Tuesday."

"Honey, you know how you were made, right? It was not by immaculate conception, you know." The smile in my mom's voice makes me smile as well. I miss her. It's been so long since I've seen her happy.

I'd driven to Alpenglow Ridge in a blaze of tears and panic, thinking I only had a sliver of a chance to see my dad again. The drive is just over an hour away. Each second moved at a glacial pace. I had her on speakerphone in my car for the entire drive. Neither of us said anything. The sounds of the bustling hospital whirred over the sound of my tires ripping the highway up. The cold from that lobby waiting room followed me from the hospital for weeks after.

I couldn't shake that chill.

To hear her smile again, erases that guilt I had felt for coming back to Denver. They were more than surviving in my absence. There's no way I can be in Alpenglow Ridge for long stretches of time since I left. It's too risky.

But this smile. This small little bit of happiness in her voice is enough to make me smile too. Still, I can't picture myself even packing that suitcase I've laid out on my floor now without remembering the last fateful time that I tried to pack it up. Going back to Alpenglow Ridge is probably the dumbest thing I could imagine doing.

It's not smart. And in most things, I would consider myself to be smart. Except when I was younger and made the worst decision, over and over and over again.

"Mom, please." I start grabbing clothes from my laundry basket and throw them into the luggage. From the clean clothes basket, instead of my dirty clothes laundry basket, of course.

"I want to know why dad couldn't call me. Why can't he just call me like you're doing now and tell me what's up?" I walk into my small bathroom across the open studio space. "Toothbrush, toothpaste, face wash, face creams, toner…" The ones *he* preferred ran out a long time ago. I could likely repurchase the bottles I'm packing all for under fifty dollars. But, I don't have fifty dollars to spare.

I throw them into my smaller toiletry bag. My eyes snag on the gold wrappers sticking out from the bathroom drawer. It's not like I've needed them for months. I pick up the roll of condoms considering how necessary it would be to pack.

Why second guess? Better safe than sorry.

"Honey, I don't know what your dad wants. Only that he asked me to get you up here. I take it that you're packing so I can tell him you're on the way, right?"

I brush through my extensions. The tangled mess I woke up with is almost untamable since I went to sleep without my scarf on last night. *Scary.* A little hair oil couldn't hurt. I rub some argan oil in my hands before smoothing it over my blonde ends. It almost looks perfect.

Plugging in my straightener, I answer my mom, "Yea, I guess. I'm working a double on Friday. I'm not staying long." I press the straightener over my hair, flipping the ends just how I like them. "Tell him that because I don't want the guilt trip."

She chuckles. "Of course. Because that's going to do something. Your dad has his own plans. I'll have breakfast waiting for you, honey."

I hang up after we exchange I *love yous* and stare at my phone a little longer.

I'm going to Alpenglow Ridge. Fine. Just a few days. No big deal. He'll never know. I repeat it in my head as I carefully apply makeup and lashes.

Shoes are the last thing to get thrown into my suitcase. My tank top and skinny jeans are cute enough for the ranch. But my chucks? Oh no.

Definitely need my boots.

These wine-red cowboy boots were a present from mom. It's been a few years and I only wore them on the ranch a few times before they sat here useless in my closet.

They aren't who I am anymore.

I shrug to myself in the full-length mirror on my wall. Turning to get a view of my backside, I do a little twerk. Confirming, "It's still fat, baby!" I smack my ass and blow a kiss to myself. All the happy times with my friends and family are taped along the edges of this mirror. Including the photo I posted yesterday.

I focus on the one I took after Mel's twenty-first birthday party. We had spent the better part of that weekend miserably hungover, but it was the best night. It's been a while since we all hung out. Things aren't the same anymore. On the off chance I spend some time in town there, I've decided to throw in something other than tank tops... just in case.

Satisfied with what I've packed, I drag my small suitcase down all three flights of stairs. I'm Alpenglow Ridge bound.

Saddled with Finesse

Chapter 2 – Cory

"It's not fair for our teachers to stay here longer than they are expected to. The school year is almost over and they are tired, Mr. Whitfield." *I'm tired.*

"I know, it's my wi—their mother's day to pick them up and I guess she just forgot or something. I'm coming as quickly as I can. Give me fifteen minutes... tops! Please."

She sighs a heavy sound that presses down on my shoulders. I try my best to be safe, but also quick, making it through rush hour traffic in Denver. "Fifteen minutes, Mr. Whitfield."

I arrive at the school in fourteen minutes where Cory Jr. and Brendan are sitting on the curb in the pickup line. Their vice-principal, Alison Blackburn, waits behind them with her arms crossed. I park and get out of the car to open the back door of my truck for them. I'm fully prepared to give her the long speech. The one about how I'm trying to make things work with the custody agreement I have with their mom. I still haven't been able to get in touch with her and she didn't tell me that she couldn't make it to pick up the kids today.

My mouth opens to begin my story, but Alison holds up a hand. "It's fine, Mr. Whitfield. They're good kids and were no trouble at all, but you must find a way to prevent this from happening so often. I've made a note in your file about it, but with just three days left of school, I'm certain you can figure it out." She gives me a stern look with an eyebrow raised. Her teacher's tone makes me feel like a chastised student... instead of a thirty-year-old man who is drowning in his own life.

I nod. "Yes, of course." She nods back to me and heads over to her car, parked behind where I pulled up and drives off like a bat out of hell. When I turn back to my truck, CJ gives me a lopsided tilt of his lips. I scrub a hand over my neck. I have no idea what to tell them. None of this conversation should be happening in this after-school pickup line. I hustle back to the driver's side and check my rearview. "Everybody buckled?"

"Yep" they both respond. Bren from his booster and CJ from the other side of the car seat for my youngest.

"Alright. Let's hit it." The daycare that Gabriel, my two, almost three, year old is at stays open until six for pick up. It's five-thirty, so I should make it there well before they close. It's only around the corner from my two oldest's elementary school. "How was taekwondo?" I look at them in the rearview again.

"Today was the last day. We just had a party to celebrate," CJ responds.

"That sounds like fun. Was there cake?"

"No cake. But we got juice and snacks! They had my favorite rainbow Goldfish, dad!" Bren adds in with a bounce. He pulls, a now crumpled, piece of paper from his backpack. "And our certificates of completion! Can we hang it up in the living room?"

Before I can reply, CJ speaks up. "That means we will need to be picked up at three-thirty tomorrow... And Thursday and Friday." He reminds me, just a hint of bitterness in his tone. My heart squeezes at being judged by my oldest. He knows too much. Has felt the hurt of our separation the fiercest, as well.

"I know, son. I know." I consider throwing Vanessa under the bus like I very well deserve to do. That doesn't change the fact that my kids were the last ones to be picked up today. I keep my mouth closed.

We arrive at Sunshine Tots with time to spare and I get my toddler situated in his car seat.

Back at home, my phone vibrates on the dining table. I ordered something to be delivered for dinner when I acknowledged there was nothing in the fridge worth trying to combine for an actual meal. The screen shows a picture of my aunt Janet and me when I was eighteen. I smile with my whole face as she looks down at me. I pick up, saying, "Hey, auntie."

"Hey, Cory. How are you?"

Considering how to respond, I go with the truth. "I'm tired as hell. What about you?"

"I've been better. You know what today is?"

It takes me a second, but I realize that today is *that* day. The day that changed my life forever. "How can it be that twenty years have passed?"

"I don't know, but I miss her every day. Even your dad too." She pauses like she's choosing her next words with care. "You doing okay?"

I scoff, wiping a tear she can probably hear in my voice but I respond, "Yea. I'm good." I look in on the boys getting ready for bed. Bren and CJ are following their routines and Gabe sits happily in the room on the floor in his pajamas. He's rolling a truck on the carpeted rug that looks like a series of roads overlapping all in dizzying patterns. Stepping back into the kitchen, I start putting away to-go containers and wiping the table down.

"You sure?"

I sigh. "No. I'm not, but I'm too tired to think about something else that I need to be handling better. Van forgot to pick up the boys from school. I have to give away two of my properties this week because I can't chance that she will forget them again. I have no idea what I'm going to do with the boys when school is out. Somehow, I forgot to find some sort of activity or camp or something for them. I've been up since four this morning. I'm tired, Jan. I'm really fucking tired."

"You can always come home." *Home.* My aunt moved to Alpenglow Ridge about ten years ago after I graduated from high school. She's built a life there. Found the love of her life, Sammie, and seems happy. Hell, I'm happy for her. But... "I don't know if that's a good idea."

"And why not? You say that every time I suggest it. The boys will be out of school. I know you're paying that condo month to month. Denver is still the worst place to buy a home. Just give them the proper notice and come stay with me."

"I can't just leave, Jan. How am I supposed to feed my boys or myself with no job? We'll eat you out of your house and home. We would be too big of a burden on you there. You do remember I have three kids right?"

"And I have three guest rooms. How is that any different from your condo there? As far as work goes, you think Alpenglow doesn't have lawns and such. Let me ask around, I'm sure I could get you something started."

Could moving in with my aunt be a good idea? There are so many reasons why it could be. For one, I need a damn break. A full day of hauling soil bags, digging holes, sweating in the sun... trying to make everyone else look like they have the picture-perfect house. It's as much as I can take.

Vanessa still hasn't responded to any of my texts or calls. How do you... Just forget to pick up your own children? I mean really... What the hell? She doesn't want to be with me? Fine. Our marriage was not the best thing in my life, but it was ours. She wanted out, I let her go. But the boys? She can't decide to be in and out whenever she feels like it. I'm there for them in the good and bad times.

I'm not usually one to complain, but I'm reaching a breaking point.

"It'll give you a break and you can start somewhere fresh. I work from home, I can watch the boys for you. I miss my littles anyway. Christmas was so long ago and I came to you all." I start to respond and tell her all the reasons that I think this is a bad idea. But, she's right. A break sounds nice.

"I don't know, Jan."

"What about starting your own landscaping company? That used to be your dream, the goal. Is it not anymore?"

I had been working for Mark for the past five years. It's nice to have a little bit of direction in what and where I go day to day. I love not having to think about anything. I simply show up and do my job. It's easy.

What if I did have help though? Starting my own business could be...

"It is something I want. I want that very much so. But I don't know. Janet, that's a lot of work. And with the boys..."

"I said I've got them. Only until you figure it out."

"I'll think about it."

"I love you, nephew."

"I love you. Listen, I need to finish putting the boys to bed. I'll call you later okay?"

"Take me in there so I can say goodnight on speaker."

I do what she asks and let her go.

Laying in bed that night, I think over her proposal again. It's not that far-fetched of an idea.

Reaching into my nightstand, I pull out the old worn envelope and look it over. The edges have long been rubbed away. The small sticker that used to keep it closed is no longer sticky, but I've since used Cellatape to hold it in place.

To my son on his birthday,

First, I love you. You are the best present that your father and I ever received. How lucky is it, that on my birthday, I gave birth to you? We are so blessed to have you in our lives. Everyday that we get to watch you grow has been the best day ever. Never forget that you are loved and will always have someone on your team as long as we are around. Our wish for you is to keep that love in your heart for your friends, your family and this earth. We know you will make us so proud this year! Your dad says that he still expects you to make the honor roll. I do not doubt that you will. The big 1-0! Enjoy your party tonight and make a splash!

All our love,

Mama and Daddy

I stare at the ceiling for a few minutes. Wiping the tears from my eyes, I return the card back to its spot. The last handwritten thing I ever received from them. How many times have I read it? Vanessa never understood why I still held onto their memory so tightly. But how could she? She's never lost anyone.

It's only me who is always losing. My life—a series of losses. People don't seem to stick around as far as I'm concerned.

Seems like the best thing for me is to go where I can have even the smallest bit of support. To be closer to my remaining family. I've got a bit saved away. Not enough for long, but enough to make it work for a few months. I've made up my mind. Come Monday, I'm putting in my two weeks. Alpenglow Ridge, here we come.

KEEP READING CORY AND REESE'S STORY, **SADDLED WITH FINESSE**, HERE!

Saddled
with
Finesse

Acknowledgements

Thank you to my husband and daughter for being patient and encouraging with me as I continue to write these stories. I love you both so much more than words can say!

Thank you to Faith H, Karime G and my other BETA readers! You ladies are rockstars! I am always so grateful for your feedback! Big hugs!

Thank you to my returning readers for showing your support and engaging with my stories!

Thank you to my new readers! I hope you enjoyed and will stick around for more stories!

Keep up to date with me and all my new releases by signing up for my newsletter:

www.zeakayleighgalan.com/news

Also by Zea Kayleigh Galan

Alpenglow Ridge

Saddled with Finesse
Verse to Acclimate
Whisk til Peaked
Hope by the Horizon
Roped on the Ridge

About the Author

Zea is a passionate storyteller who brings small-town romance to life with heartfelt emotion and unforgettable characters. A lifelong lover of love stories, she weaves her background in anthropology into crafting tales where swoon-worthy heroes fall hard for their strong, relatable heroines.

Living in the picturesque mountains of Colorado with her husband, daughter, and a spoiled, posh cat, Zea draws inspiration from her surroundings to create warm, vibrant settings readers want to escape to. When she's not writing, she's indulging in her other loves: cooking, hiking, designing clothes, or curling up with a romance novel and a plate of sweets.

Zea is dedicated to connecting with her readers and invites you to join her on this journey of love, laughter, and happily ever afters.

Want to be the first to hear about new releases, exclusive content, and special offers?

Sign up for my newsletter at
www.zeakayleighgalan.com/news.
www.instagram.com/zeakayleigh
www.facebook.com/zeakayleigh
Signed Book Shop